Gerda In Sweden

By

Etta Blaisdell Mcdonald

Gerda In Sweden
by Etta Blaisdell Mcdonald

ISBN: 978-93-61421-00-6

Published by

DOUBLE 9 BOOKS

2/13-B, Ansari Road
Daryaganj, New Delhi – 110002
info@double9books.com
www.double9books.com
Tel. 011-40042856

ABOUT THE AUTHOR

Etta Blaisdell McDonald was an American novelist recognized for her enthralling children's novels that transported young readers to exotic locations and introduced them to other cultures. One of her most cherished works is "Gerda in Sweden," a lovely story that transports readers to Scandinavia's breathtaking scenery and rich customs. In "Gerda in Sweden," McDonald tells a beautiful story of a young girl named Gerda who sets out to see Sweden's picturesque countryside. Readers are taken on a journey through the beauty of Sweden's natural beauties, from lush woods and sparkling lakes to quaint villages and breathtaking mountains, thanks to Gerda. As Gerda travels through the Swedish countryside, she meets a variety of fascinating folks, each with their own distinct story and customs. Along the process, she learns important lessons about friendship, courage, and the value of trying new things. McDonald's rich descriptions and compelling narration transport readers to a world of surprise and discovery, with every page brimming with Swedish sights, sounds, and smells.

CONTENTS

PREFACE

The Swedish people are a hospitable, peace-loving race, kindly and industrious, making the most of their resources. In the south of Sweden are broad farming-lands with well-tilled fields and comfortable red farmhouses; in the central portion are hills and dales, rich in mines of copper and iron which have been famous for hundreds of years. In the cities and towns are factories where thousands of workers are employed, making all sorts of useful articles, from matches to steam-engines. The rivers which flow down to the sea from the western chain of mountains carry millions of logs from the great dark forests. As soon as the ice breaks up in the spring, whole fleets of fishing boats and lumber vessels sail up and down the coast; sawmills whirr and buzz all day long; the hum of labor is heard all over the land.

In this Northland the winter days are short and cold; but there are the long sunny summer days, when even in the south of Sweden midnight is nothing but a soft twilight, and in the north the sun shines for a whole month without once dipping below the horizon. This is a glorious time for both young and old. The people live out-of-doors day and night, going to the parks and gardens, rowing and sailing and swimming, singing and dancing on the village green, celebrating the midsummer festival with feasting and merry-making,—for once more the sun rides high in the heavens, and Baldur, the sun god, has conquered the frost giants.

Just such a happy, useful life is found in this little story. Gerda and her twin brother take a trip northward across the Baltic Sea with their father, who is an inspector of lighthouses. On their way they meet Karen, a little lame girl. After going farther north, into Lapland, where they see the sun shining at midnight, and spend a day with a family of Lapps and their reindeer, Gerda takes Karen home to Stockholm with her so that the child may have the benefit of the famous Swedish gymnastics for her lameness. Then such good times as the three children have together! They go to the winter carnival to see the skating and skiing; they celebrate Yule-tide with all the good old Swedish customs; and there is a birthday party for the twins, when Karen also receives a gift,—the very best gift of all.

CHAPTER I
GERDA AND BIRGER

If any one had stopped to think of it, the ticking of the tall clock that stood against the wall sounded like "Ger-da! Ger-da!"

But no one did stop to think of it. Everyone was far too busy to think about the clock and what it was saying, for over in the corner beside the tall stove stood a wooden cradle, and in the cradle were two tiny babies.

There they lay, side by side, in the same blue-painted cradle that had rocked the Ekman babies for over two hundred years; and one looked so exactly like the other that even dear Grandmother Ekman could not tell them apart.

But the mother, who rocked them so gently and watched them so tenderly, touched one soft cheek and then another, saying proudly, "This is our son, and this is our daughter," even when both pairs of blue eyes were tightly closed, and both little chins were tucked under the warm blanket.

There is always great rejoicing over the coming of new babies in any family; but there was twice as much rejoicing as usual over these babies, and that was because they were twins.

Little Ebba Jorn and her brother Nils came with their mother, from the farm across the lake, to see the blue-eyed babies in the worn blue cradle; and after them came all the other neighbors, so that there was always some one in the big chair beside the cradle, gazing admiringly at the twins.

It was in March that they were born,—bleak March, when snow covered the ground and the wind whistled down the broad chimney; when the days were cold and the nights colder; when the frost giants drove their horses, the fleet frost-winds, through the valleys, and cast their spell over lakes and rivers.

April came, and then May. The sun god drove the frost giants back into their dark caves, the trees shook out their tender, green leaves, and flowers blossomed in the meadows. But still the tall clock ticked away the days, and still they questioned, "What shall we name the babies?"

"Karen is a pretty name," suggested little Ebba Jorn, who had come again to see the twins, this time with a gift of two tiny knitted caps.

"My father's name is Oscar," said Nils. "That is a good name for a boy."

"It is always hard to find just the right name for a new baby," said Grandmother Ekman.

"And the task is twice as hard when there are two babies," added the proud father, laying his hand gently upon one small round head.

"Let us name the boy 'Birger' for your father," suggested his wife, kneeling beside the cradle; "and call the girl 'Anna' for your mother."

But Grandmother Ekman shook her head. "No, no!" she said decidedly. "Call the boy 'Birger' if you will; but 'Anna' is not the right name for the girl."

Anders Ekman took his hand from the baby's head to put it upon his wife's shoulder. "Here in Dalarne we have always liked your own name, Kerstin," he said with a smile.

"No maid by the name of Kerstin was ever handy with her needle," she objected. "It has always been a great trial to your mother that I have not the patience to stitch endless seams and make rainbow skirts. Our son shall be Birger; but we must think of a better name for the little daughter."

"It is plain that we shall never find two names to suit everyone," replied the father, laughing so heartily that both babies opened their big blue eyes and puckered up their lips for a good cry.

"Hush, Birger! Hush, little daughter!" whispered their mother; and she rocked the cradle gently, singing softly:—

> "Hist, hist!
> Mother is crooning and babies list.
> Hist, hist!
> The dewdrop lies in the flower's cup,
> Mother snuggles the babies up.
>   Birdie in the tree-top,
>   Do not spill the dewdrop.
> Cat be still, and dog be dumb;
> Sleep to babies' eyelids come!"

Nils and Ebba Jorn tiptoed across the room and closed the door carefully behind them. Anders Ekman took up some wood-carving and went quietly to work; while Grandmother Ekman selected a well-worn book from the book-shelf, and seated herself in the big chair by the window to look over the Norse legends of the gods and giants.

She turned the pages slowly until she found the pleasant tale of Frey, who married Gerd, the beautiful daughter of one of the frost giants. This was her favorite story, and she began reading it aloud in a low voice, while the fire burned cheerfully on the hearth, and the cradle swayed lightly to and fro.

"Njörd, who was the god of the sea, had a son, Frey, and a daughter, Freyja. Frey was the god of the seed-time and harvest, and he brought peace and prosperity to all the world.

"In summer he gathered gentle showers and drove them up from the sea to sprinkle the dry grass; he poured warm sunshine over the hills and valleys, and ripened the fruits and grains for a bountiful harvest.

"The elves of light were his messengers, and he sent them flying about all day,—shaking pollen out of the willow tassels, filling the flower-cups with nectar, sowing the seeds, and threading the grass with beads of dew.

"But in the winter, when the frost giants ruled the earth, Frey was idle and lonely; and he rode up and down in Odin's hall on the back of his boar, Golden Bristles, longing for something to do.

"One morning, as he wandered restlessly through the beautiful city of Asgard, the home of the gods, he stood before the throne of Odin, the All-father, and saw that it was empty. 'Why should I not sit upon that throne, and look out over all the world?' he thought; and although no one but Odin was ever allowed to take the lofty seat, Frey mounted the steps and sat upon the All-father's throne.

"He looked out over Asgard, shining in the morning light, and saw the gods busy about their daily tasks. He gazed down upon the earth, with its rugged mountains and raging seas, and saw men hurrying this way and that, like tiny ants rushing out of their hills.

"Last of all he turned his eyes toward distant Jötunheim, the dark, forbidding home of the frost giants; but in that gloomy land of ice and snow he could see no bright nor beautiful thing. Great black cliffs stood like sentinels along the coast, dark clouds hung over the hills, and cold winds swept through the valleys.

"At the foot of one of the hills stood a barren and desolate dwelling, alone in all that dark land of winter; and as Frey gazed, a maiden came slowly through the valley and mounted the steps to the entrance of the house.

"Then, as she raised her arms to open the door, suddenly the sky, and sea, and all the earth were flooded with a bright light, and Frey saw that she was the most beautiful maiden in the whole world."

Kerstin looked up at her husband and spoke quickly. "That is like the coming of our two babies," she said. "In the days of ice and snow they brought light and gladness to our hearts. Let us call the sweet daughter 'Gerda' after the goddess of sunshine and happiness."

So the two babies were named at last. When the children of the neighborhood heard of it, they flocked to the house with their hands full of gifts, dancing round and round the cradle and singing a merry song that made the rafters ring. The wheels of thin Swedish bread that hung over the stove shook on their pole, the tall clock ticked louder than ever, and the twins opened their blue eyes and smiled their sweetest smile at so much happiness.

But they were not very strong babies, so Anders Ekman went off to his work in Stockholm and left them in Dalarne with their mother and grandmother, hoping that the good country air would make them plump and sturdy.

Dalarne, or the Dales, is the loveliest part of all Sweden, and the Ekman farm lay on the shore of a lake so beautiful that it is often called the "Eye of Dalarne."

It was in the Dales that Gerda and little Birger outgrew their cradle and their baby clothes, and became the sturdy children their father longed to have them.

When they were seven years old their mother took them to live in Stockholm; but with each new summer they hurried away from the city with its schools and lessons, to spend the long vacation at the farm.

"Gerda and Birger are here!" they would cry, opening the door and running into the living-room to find their grandmother.

"Gerda and Birger are here!" The news always ran through the neighborhood in a twinkling, and from far and near the boys and girls flocked down the road to bid them welcome.

"Ger-da! Ger-da!" the old clock in the corner ticked patiently, just as it had been ticking for eleven long years. But who could listen to it now? There were flowers and berries to pick, chickens to feed, and games to play, through all the long summer days in Dalarne. Surely, Gerda and Birger had no time to listen to the clock.

CHAPTER II
THE SURPRISE BOX

All day long the gentle breezes blowing through the city streets, and the bright sun shining on the sparkling water of Lake Mälar, called to the children that spring had come in Stockholm.

Great cakes of ice went floating through the arches of the bridge across the Norrström, and gray gulls, sailing up from the bay, darted down to the swirling water to find dainty morsels for their dinner.

The little steamers which had been lying idly at the quays all winter were being scraped and painted, and made ready for their summer's work; children were playing in the parks; throngs of people filled the streets;— spring was in the air!

But in the Ekman household Gerda and Birger had been as busy as bees all day, with no thought for the dancing blue water and the shining blue sky. Their tongues had flown fast, their fingers faster; they had hunted up old clothes, old books, old games; and had added one package after another to the contents of a big box that stood in the corner of the pleasant living-room.

"Perhaps I can finish this needle-book, if I hurry," said Gerda, drawing her chair up to the window to catch the light from the setting sun.

"I wanted to send this work-box, too," added Birger; "but how can I carve an initial on the cover when I don't know who is going to have the box?"

"Carve an 'F' for friend," suggested Gerda, stopping to thread her needle; but just then there was a sound of chattering voices on the stairs, and work-box and needle-book were forgotten.

As Birger sprang to open the door, a little mob of happy boys and girls burst into the room with a shout of heartiest greeting. Their eyes were sparkling with fun, their cheeks rosy from a run in the fresh spring air, and their arms were filled with bundles of all sizes and shapes.

"Ho, Birger! Oh, Gerda!" was their cry; "it took us an endless time to get past the porter's wife at the street door, and she made us answer a dozen questions. 'To what apartment were we going? Whom did we wish to see? Why did we all come together?'"

"And did you tell her that you were coming to the third apartment to see the Ekman twins, and were bringing clothing and gifts to fill a surprise box?" asked Gerda, holding up her apron for the packages.

"Yes," replied a jolly, round-faced boy whom the others called Oscar, "and we had to explain that we didn't know who was to have the box, nor why you telephoned to us to bring the gifts to-night, when you said only last week that you wouldn't want them until the first of June."

"There has been a hard storm on the northern coast, and Father is going by train as far as Luleå, to see if it did much damage to the lighthouses," Gerda explained. "He thinks that the storm may have caused great suffering among the poor people, so we are going to send our box with him, instead of waiting to send it by boat in June. He has to start on his trip very early in the morning, so the box must be ready to-night."

Everyone began talking at once, and a tall girl with pretty curly hair, who had something important to say, had to raise her voice above the din before she could be heard. "Let us write a letter and put it into the box with the gifts," she suggested.

"Ja så! Yes, of course! That is good!" they all cried; and while Gerda ran to get pen and ink, the boys and girls gathered around a table that stood in the center of the room.

"Dear Yunker Unknown:—" began a mischievous-looking boy, pretending to write with a great flourish.

"Nonsense!" cried Sigrid Lundgren. "The box is filled with skirts and aprons and caps and embroidered belts, and all sorts of things for a girl. Don't call her Yunker. Yunker means farmer."

"Well, then, 'Dear Jungfru Unknown:—'" the boy corrected, with more flourishes.

"I wish we knew who would get the box, then we should know just what to say," said little Hilma Berling.

"She is probably just your age, and is named Selma," said Birger; and everyone laughed over his choice of a name.

"Yes," agreed Oscar, "and she lives in the depths of the white northern forests, with only a white polar bear and a white snowy owl for company."

"I don't believe we shall ever be able to write a letter," said Birger, shaking his head. "How can we write to some one we have never seen?"

and he sat himself down on a red painted cricket beside the tall stove and began carving the cover of the work-box.

"We have made all the little gifts in that box for some one we have never seen," said Sigrid. "It ought to be just as easy to write her a letter."

"No, Sigrid," Birger told her; "it is the hardest thing in the world to write a letter, especially if you have nothing to say. I would rather make a box and carve it, than write half of a letter."

"Here comes Mother. She will tell us what to write," said Gerda.

"Why not write about some of the good times you have together here in Stockholm," suggested her mother, and she took up the pen and waited for some one to start the letter.

"Our dear Girl-friend in the North:—" said Hilma for a beginning; and as Fru Ekman wrote at their dictation, first one and then another added a message, until finally she leaned back in her chair and told them to listen to what she had written.

"We are a club of capital boys and girls because we live in Sweden's capital city," she began.

"That was from Oscar," interrupted Gerda; but her mother continued,— "and we send you this box for a surprise.

"We go to school and have to study very hard; but we find a little time for play every day. Sometimes we go to the park, but when it storms we are glad to stay in the house and work at sewing or sloyd. So, ever since Yuletide, we have been making little gifts for you,—the girls with their needles, the boys with their saws and knives.

"We hope you will enjoy wearing the caps and aprons as much as we have enjoyed making them; and if you have a brother, please give him the watch and the leather watch-chain. It is a gift from Oscar.

"The rainbow skirt is one which Gerda wore last summer. She has outgrown it now, and will have to have a new one next year. She hopes it is not too small for you.

"If you want to know what Stockholm is like, you must think of islands and bridges, because the city is built on eight islands, and they are all connected by bridges with each other and with the mainland. In summer, little steamers go around the city, in and out among the islands; but in winter the lake and all the bays are frozen over, and there is good skating everywhere.

"Then you should see the twelve girls and boys who are writing this letter, holding fast to one another in a long line, and skimming across Djurgården bay or skating around Stadenholm, where the King's Palace stands.

"Sometime, if you will come to visit us in Stockholm, we will have you join the line and skate with us under the bridges, and up and down the waterways; and we will show you what good times we can have in the city."

"So we did write a letter after all," sighed Birger, as Fru Ekman finished reading. "Now we must sign our names;" and after much discussion and laughter the twelve names appeared on the paper, written in a circle without any beginning or end,—Sigrid's and Hilma's and Oscar's and Gerda's and all.

"Put it in the box and we'll nail on the cover," cried Oscar, picking up the hammer and pounding as if he were driving a dozen nails at once.

"Can't a poor man read his newspaper in peace, without being disturbed by all this noise?" called Herr Ekman from the next room; but when he appeared in the doorway the merry twinkle in his eyes showed that he cared little about the noise and was glad to see the children having a good time.

"I'd like to be going north with this box," said Magnus, as he took some nails and began nailing on the cover.

"Father goes every summer to inspect the lighthouses along the coast," said Birger, "and he has promised to take me with him sometime."

"And me, too," added Gerda; "he wouldn't take you without me."

"Is it very different in the far North?" asked Oscar.

"Yes," replied Herr Ekman, "the winter is long and cold and dark; there are severe storms, and deep snow covers the ground; but the boys and girls find plenty to do, and seem to be just as happy as you are," and he pinched Oscar's ear as he spoke.

"I don't see how they can be happy in the winter when it is dark all night and almost all day," said Olaf.

Herr Ekman laughed. "Do you think they should go into a den, like the bears, and sleep through the winter?" he asked.

"But think of the summer, when it is light all day and all night, too," said Sigrid. "Then they have fun enough to make up for the winter."

"I never could understand about our long nights in winter and our long days in summer," spoke Hilma Berling.

"It is because we live so near the North Pole," Oscar told her. "Now that Commander Peary of the United States of America has really discovered the North Pole, perhaps the geographies will make it easier to understand how the sun juggles with the poles and circles.

"I am sorry that it has been discovered," he added. "I always meant to do it myself, when I got old enough to discover anything."

"If I could stand on the top of Mount Dundret and see the sun shining at midnight, I am sure I could understand about it without any geography," Gerda declared.

"If you should go north with Herr Lighthouse-Inspector Ekman this summer, you might meet the little girl who receives this box," said Sigrid.

"I should know her the minute I saw her," Gerda said decidedly.

"How would you know her?" questioned Birger. "You don't even know her name or where she lives. Father is going to give the box to the lighthouse-master at Luleå, and he will decide where to send it."

"Oh, there are ways!" replied Gerda. "And besides, she would have on my rainbow skirt."

That night, after the children had trooped down the stairs and away to their homes, and after Gerda and Birger had said good-night and gone to their beds, the father and mother sat by the table, talking over plans for the summer.

"I suppose we shall start for Dalarne the day after school closes," suggested Fru Ekman.

"No," answered her husband, "I have been thinking that the children are old enough now to travel a little; and I have decided to take them with me when I go north this summer. They ought to know more about the forests, and rivers, and shores of their good old Mother Svea."

CHAPTER III
ON BOARD THE "NORTH STAR"

It was a sunny morning in late June. The waters of the Saltsjö rippled and sparkled around the islands of Stockholm, and little steamers puffed briskly about in the harbor. The tide had turned, and the fresh water of the lake, mingled with the salt water of the fjord, was swirling and eddying under the bridges and beating against the stone quays; for Lake Mälar is only eighteen inches higher than the Salt Sea, and while the incoming tide brings salt water up the river from the ocean, the outgoing tide carries fresh water down from the lake.

Just as the great clock in the church tower began chiming the hour of nine, a group of children gathered on the granite pier opposite the King's Palace.

A busy scene greeted their eyes. Vessels were being loaded and unloaded, passengers were arriving, men were hurrying to and fro, and boys selling newspapers were rushing about in the crowd.

"Do you see the *North Star*?" Sigrid asked the others. "That is the name of the boat they are going to take."

"There it is!" cried Oscar; "and there are Gerda and Birger on the deck." With a merry shout of greeting he ran on board the steam launch, followed by all the other girls and boys.

"Oh, Gerda, how I wish I were going with you," said Hilma wistfully. "I should love to cross the Arctic Circle and see the sun shining all night long."

Gerda, who was wearing a pretty blue travelling dress, with blue ribbons on her hat and in her hair, threw her arms around her friend. "I wish you were going, too," she answered. "Birger is the best brother any girl could have; but he isn't like a sister, and that is what you are to me, Hilma."

At the same moment, Birger was confiding to his friend, "I wish you were going with us, Oscar. Gerda is a good sister; but she isn't like a brother."

All the other boys and girls were talking and laughing together, telling of the strange sights that Birger and Gerda would see on their trip into Lapland; and what they would do if only they were going, too.

Suddenly a warning whistle from the steamer sent them hurrying back to the quay, where they stood waving their handkerchiefs and shouting good wishes until the twins were out of sight.

The vessel's course lay first between two islands, and Gerda lifted her eyes to the windows of the King's Palace, which stood near the quay of one; but Birger found more to interest him in the military and naval buildings on the other.

"There is a ship from Liverpool, England," said Lieutenant Ekman, pointing to a vessel which was lying beside the quay in front of the palace.

"It is hard to believe that we are forty miles from the ocean when we see such big ships in our harbor," said Birger. "How did it happen that Stockholm was built so far from the open sea? It would be easier for all these vessels if they didn't have to come sailing up among all the islands to find a landing-place."

"Lake Mälar was the stronghold of the ancient Viking warriors," replied his father; "and it was just because there were forty miles of difficult sailing among narrow channels, that they chose to live at the head of the Saltsjö, and make this fjord their thoroughfare in going out to the Baltic Sea."

"Did they like to make things as hard as possible for themselves?" asked Gerda with interest.

"Not so much as they liked to make it as hard as possible for their enemies," said Herr Ekman. "Centuries ago, hunters and fishermen built their rude huts on the wooded islands at the outlet of Mälar Lake. They often found it convenient to slip away from their pursuers among these islands; but they were not always successful, for their settlements on the site of the present city were repeatedly destroyed by hostile tribes."

"Why didn't they build fortifications on the islands and hold the enemy at bay?" questioned Birger.

"They were too busy sailing off to foreign lands," answered his father. "Fleet after fleet of Viking ships sailed out of the bays of Sweden, manned by the bravest sailors the world has ever known; and they swooped down upon the tribes of Europe, fighting and conquering them with the strength of giants and the glee of children."

"It was Birger Jarl who built the first walls and towers to protect the city," spoke Gerda. "I remember learning it in my history lesson."

"Yes," her father replied; "good old Earl Birger, who ruled the Swedes in the thirteenth century, saw how important such fortifications would be, and so he locked up the Mälar Lake from hostile fleets by building walls and towers around one of the islands and making it his capital."

"There is an old folk-song in one of my books which always reminds me of the Vikings," said Birger.

"Let us hear it," suggested his father, and Birger repeated:—

> "Brave of heart and warriors bold,
> Were the Swedes from time untold;
> Breasts for honor ever warm,
> Youthful strength in hero arm.
>> Blue eyes bright
>> Dance with light
> For thy dear green valleys old.
> North, thou giant limb of earth,
> With thy friendly, homely hearth."

"There is another stanza," said Gerda. "I like the second one best," and she added:—

> "Song of many a thousand year
> Rings through wood and valley clear;
> Picture thou of waters wild,
> Yet as tears of mourning mild.
>> To the rhyme
>> Of past time
> Blend all hearts and lists each ear.
> Guard the songs of Swedish lore,
> Love and sing them evermore."

"Good," said Lieutenant Ekman; "isn't there a third stanza, Birger?"

But Birger was at the other end of the boat. "Come here, Gerda," he called. "We can see Waxholm now."

Then, as the boat slipped past the great fortress and began to thread its way in and out among the islands in the fjord, the twins stood at the rail, pointing out to each other a beautiful wooded island, a windmill, a rocky ledge, a pretty summer cottage nestling among the trees, a fisherman's hut with fishing nets hung up on poles to dry, an eagle soaring across the blue sky, or a flock of terns flying up from the rocks with their harsh, rattling cry.

There was a new and interesting sight every moment, and the sailors in their blue uniforms nodded to each other with pleasure as Gerda flitted across the deck.

"She is like a little bluebird," they said; and like a bird she chirped and twittered, singing snatches of song, and asking a hundred questions.

"I like those old fancies that the Vikings had about the sea and the sky and the winds," she said at last, stretching her arms wide and dancing from end to end of the deck. "They called the sea the 'necklace of the earth,' and the sky the 'wind-weaver.'"

"I wish I had the magic boat that Loki gave to Frey," answered Birger lazily, lying flat on his back and looking up into the "wind-weaver." "If I had it, I would sail over the whole long 'necklace of the earth,' from clasp to clasp."

But Gerda was already out of hearing. She had gone to sit beside her father and watch the course of the boat through the thousands of rocky islands that stud the coast.

"The captain says that the frost giants threw all these rocks out here when they were having a battle with old Njord, the god of the sea," she said. Then, as she caught sight of a lighthouse on a low outer ledge,—"Why, Father!" she cried, "I thought we were going to stop at every lighthouse on the coast."

"So we are, after we leave the Skärgård," replied Lieutenant Ekman. "I came down as far as this several weeks ago when the ice went out of the fjord. There are two or three months when all this water is frozen over and there can be no shipping; but as soon as the ice breaks up, the lamps are lighted in the lighthouses and I come down to see them. Now it is so light all night that for two months the lamps are not lighted at all unless there is a storm."

Gerda ran to the rail to wave her handkerchief to a little girl on the deck of a lumber vessel which they were passing.

"The lighthouse keepers have a good many vacations, don't they?" she said when she came back.

"Yes," replied her father; "those on the east coast of Sweden have several months in the winter when the Baltic Sea and the Gulf of Bothnia are covered with solid ice; but on the south and west coasts the lighthouses and even the lightships are lighted all winter."

"Why is that?" questioned Birger, coming to join them.

"There is a warm current which crosses the Atlantic Ocean from the Gulf of Mexico and washes our western coast. It is called the Gulf Stream. This current warms the air and makes the climate milder, and it keeps the water from freezing, so that shipping is carried on all winter," Lieutenant Ekman explained.

Just then a sailor came to tell them that their dinner was ready. While they were eating, the launch made a landing at the first of the lighthouses which the inspector had to visit.

While their father was busy, the twins clambered over the rocks, hunting for starfishes and sea-urchins, and Gerda picked a bouquet of bright blossoms for their table on the boat.

At the next stopping-place, which was Gefle, the captain took them on shore to see the shipyard where his own launch, the *North Star*, was built; and so, all day long, there was something to keep them busy.

As the boat steamed farther north, each new day grew longer, each night shorter, until Birger declared that he believed the sun did not set at all.

"Oh, yes it does," his father told him. "It sets now at about eleven o'clock, and rises a little after one. You will have to wait until you cross the Polcirkel and get to the top of Mount Dundret before you have a night when the sun doesn't even dip below the horizon."

"We must be pretty near the Arctic Circle now," exclaimed Gerda. "It is growing colder and colder every minute."

"That is because the wind is blowing over an ice-floe," said her father, pointing to a large field of ice which seemed to be drifting slowly toward them.

"Look, look, Birger!" cried Gerda, "there are some seals on the ice."

"Yes," said Birger, "and there is a seal-boat sailing up to catch them."

"I'm going to draw a picture of it for Mother," Gerda announced, and she sat still for a long time, making first one sketch and then another,—a seal on a cake of ice, a lighthouse, a ship being dashed against the rocks, and a steam-launch cutting through the water, with a boy and girl on its deck.

"Oh dear!" she sighed after a while, "I wish something *enormous* would happen. I'm tired of water and sky and sawmills and little towns with red houses just like the pictures in my geography."

"What would you like to have happen?" questioned her father.

"I should like to see some of my girl friends," replied Gerda quickly. "I haven't had any one to tell my secrets to for over a week."

"Perhaps something enormous will happen tomorrow," her father comforted her. "We'll see what we can do about it."

So Gerda went to sleep that night thinking of Hilma and Sigrid at home; and she slept through the beautiful bright summer night, little dreaming that the boat was bearing her steadily toward a new friend and a dearer friendship than any she had ever known.

CHAPTER IV
GERDA'S NEW FRIEND

"Look, Gerda," said Lieutenant Ekman, as their launch steamed the next morning toward a barren island off the east coast of Sweden, "do you see a child on those rocks below the lighthouse?"

Gerda looked eagerly where her father pointed. "Yes, I think I see her now," she said, after a moment.

Birger ran to the bow of the boat. "Come up here," he called. "I can see her quite plainly. She has on a rainbow skirt."

"Oh, Birger!" cried Gerda, "can it be the little girl who received our box? If it is, her name is Karen. Don't you remember the letter of thanks she wrote us?"

As she spoke, the child began clambering carefully over the rocks and made her way to the landing-place. The twins saw now that she wore the rainbow skirt and the dark bodice over a white waist, which forms the costume of the Rättvik girls and women; but they saw, also, that she walked with a crutch.

"Oh, Father, she is lame!" Gerda exclaimed. Then she stood quietly on the deck, waving her hand and smiling in friendly greeting until the launch was made fast to the wharf.

"Are you Gerda?" asked the little lame girl eagerly, as Lieutenant Ekman swung his daughter ashore; and Gerda asked just as eagerly, "Are you Karen?" Then both children laughed and answered "Yes," together.

"Come up to the house, Gerda, I want to show you my birds," said Karen at once; and she climbed up over the rocks toward the tiny cottage.

Gerda followed more slowly, looking pityingly at the crutch and the poor, crooked back; but Karen turned and called to her to hurry.

"I have ever so many things to show you, Gerda," she said. "There are no children for me to play with, so I have to make friends with the birds. I have four now, and I am trying to teach them to eat from my hand."

As Karen spoke, she led the way around the corner of the house, and there, sheltered from the wind, was a collection of cages, mounted on a rough wooden bench. In each one was a bird which had been injured in some way.

The largest cage held a snowy owl, and when Karen spoke to him he ruffled up his feathers and rolled his head from side to side, his great golden eyes staring at her without blinking.

"He can't see when the sun shines," Karen explained; "but he seems to know my voice."

"What a good time he must have in the long winter nights, when he can see all the time," said Gerda. "Where did you get him?"

"Father found him in the woods with a broken wing; but he is nearly well now, and I shall soon set him free," Karen told her.

"And here is a woodpecker, and a cuckoo, and a magpie," said Gerda, looking into the cages.

"Yes," said Karen, "and last year I had an eider-duck, and I often have sea-gulls. Sometimes, when there is a big storm, the gulls are blown against the windows of the lighthouse and are hurt. I find them on the rocks in the morning with a broken leg or wing, and then I put them in a cage and take care of them until they can fly away. Father and I call this the Sea-gull Light."

"What do you do with the birds in the winter?" asked Gerda.

"The lighthouse is closed as soon as the Gulf freezes over, and then we go to live on the mainland," Karen replied. "One of my brothers built a bird-house near our barn, and if my birds are not strong enough to fly away, Father lets me take them with me in the cages, and I feed them all winter with crumbs and grain."

"How many brothers have you?"

"There are five, but they are all much older than I am. They work in the woods in the winter, cutting out logs or making tar; and in the summer they go off on fishing trips. I don't see them very often."

"We met a great many vessels loaded with lumber on our way up the coast," said Gerda, "and, wherever we stopped, the wharves were covered with great piles of lumber, and barrels and barrels of tar."

"The lumber vessels sail past this island all summer," said Karen. "I often wonder where they go, and what becomes of all the lumber they carry. There is a sawmill near our house on the shore and it whirrs and saws all day long."

"There were sawmills all along the coast," said Gerda. "Birger and I began to count them, and then there were so many other things to see that we forgot to count."

Karen stooped down to open the door of the magpie's cage, and he hopped out and began picking up the grain which she held in her hand for him. "I think this magpie is going to stay with me," she said. "He is very tame and I often let him out of the cage. Mother says he will bring me good luck," she added rather wistfully.

"It must be lonely for you here, with only the birds to play with," said Gerda. "You must be glad when the time comes to live on shore and go to school again."

For answer, Karen looked at her crutch. "I can't go to school," she said soberly; "but my brothers taught me to read and write, and Mother has a piano which I can play a little."

Then her face lighted up with a cheery smile. "When your box came this spring, it was the most exciting thing that ever happened to me. Everything in it gave me something new to think about. I often think how pretty the streets of Stockholm must look, with all the little girls going about in rainbow skirts, and none of them having to walk with a crutch."

"Oh, dear me!" exclaimed Gerda quickly; "it is not often that you see a rainbow skirt in Stockholm. I never wear one there."

Karen looked surprised. "Where do you wear it?" she asked.

Then Gerda told about her summer home in Rättvik. "It is on Lake Siljan, in the central part of Sweden, in a province that is called Dalarne," she explained. "It is a very old-fashioned place, and the people still wear the costumes which were worn hundreds of years ago."

A wistful look had stolen into Karen's face as she listened. "I suppose there are ever so many children in Rättvik," she said.

"Oh, yes," answered Gerda. "We play together every day, and go to church on Sundays; and sometimes I help to row the Sunday boat."

"What is the Sunday boat?" was Karen's next question.

"There are several parishes in Rättvik, and many of the people live so far away from the church that they row across the lake together in a long boat which is called the Sunday boat," Gerda told her.

"And do you have girl friends in Stockholm?" asked Karen, envying this Gerda who came and went from city to country so easily.

"Yes, indeed," answered Gerda. Then she smiled and said shyly, "I wish you would be my friend, too. When I go home I can write to you."

Karen's face flushed with pleasure. "Oh, will you?" she cried. "But there will be so little for me to write to you," she added soberly. "After the snow comes, and my brothers have all gone into the woods for the winter, there are weeks at a time when I never see any one but my father and mother."

"You can tell me all about your birds," Gerda suggested; "and the way the moon shines on the long stretches of snow; and about the animals that creep out from the woods sometimes and sniff around your door. And I will tell you about my school, and the parties I have with my friends. And I will send you some new music to play on the piano."

But before they could say anything more, Lieutenant Ekman had returned from inspecting the lighthouse with Karen's father, and was calling to Gerda that it was time for them to start for Luleå.

"Good-bye," the two little girls said to each other, and Karen went down to the landing-place to watch the launch steam away.

Gerda stood quietly beside the rail, looking back at the island, long after Karen's rainbow skirt and the lighthouse had faded from sight.

"I will give you two öre for your thoughts, if they are worth it," her father said at last.

"I was thinking that it will make Karen sad to hear of my good times this winter," Gerda told him.

"She will like to have your letters to think about," replied Lieutenant Ekman cheerfully. Then he pointed to a little town on the shore ahead. "There is Luleå," he said. "You will soon be travelling on the railroad toward Mount Dundret and the midnight sun."

But although Gerda was soon speeding into the mysterious Arctic regions, she could not forget her new friend in the lonely lighthouse.

CHAPTER V
CROSSING THE POLCIRKEL

"Polcirkel, Birger, Polcirkel!" cried Gerda from her side of the car.

"Polcirkel!" shouted Birger in answer, and sprang to Gerda's seat to look out of the window.

The slow-running little train groaned and creaked; then came to a stop at the tiny station-house on the Arctic Circle.

The twins, their faces smeared with vaseline and veiled in mosquito netting, hurried out of the car and looked around them. Close beside the station rose a great pile of stones, to mark the only spot where a railroad crosses the Arctic Circle. This is the most northerly railroad in the world, and was built by the Swedish government to transport iron ore to the coast, from the mines four miles north of Gellivare.

As the two children climbed to the top of the cairn, Birger said, "This is a wonderful place; is it not, Gerda?"

His sister looked back doubtfully over the immense peat bog through which the train had been travelling, and thought of the swamps and the forests of pine and birch which lay between them and Luleå, many miles away on the coast. Then she looked forward toward more peat bogs, swamps and forests that lay between them and Gellivare.

"I suppose it is a wonderful place," she said slowly; "but it seems more wonderful to me that we are here looking at it. Do you remember how it looks on the map in our geography, and how far away it always seemed?"

"Yes," replied her brother, "I always thought there was nothing but ice and snow beyond the Arctic Circle."

"So did I," said Gerda. "I had no idea we should see little farms, and fields of rye, oats and barley, away up here in Lapland. Father says the crops grow faster because the sun shines all day and almost all night, too; and that it is only eight weeks from seed-time to harvest.

"No doubt there is plenty of ice and snow in winter; but just here there seems to be nothing but swamps and forests."

"And swarms of mosquitoes," added Birger. "Don't forget the mosquitoes!"

In a moment more the children were back in their seats, and the train was creeping slowly northward, on its way toward Gellivare and Mount Dundret, where, from the fifth of June to the eleventh of July, the sun may be seen shining all day and all night.

Birger took a tiny stone from his pocket and showed it to his sister, saying, "See my souvenir of Polcirkel." But Gerda paid little attention to his souvenir, and slipped over to her father's seat to ask a question.

"Father," she said softly.

Lieutenant Ekman looked up from the maps and papers in his lap. "What do you wish, little daughter?" he asked.

"Will you please make me a promise?" she begged.

"If it won't take all my money to keep it," he answered with a smile.

But Gerda seemed in no hurry to tell what it was that she wanted, and began looking over the papers in his lap. "What is this?" she asked, taking up a small blue card.

"That is my receipt from the Tourist Agency," he answered. "When I give it to the station master at Gellivare, he will give me a key which will open the hut on Mount Dundret, and let us see the midnight sun in comfort."

"How much did you pay for it?" was Gerda's next question.

"I paid about four kronor for the card and all the privileges that go with it," was the answer.

"Have you plenty of money left?" asked the little girl.

Her father laughed. "Enough to get us all three back to Stockholm, at least," he said. "Why do you ask?"

"Because—" said Gerda slowly, and then stopped.

"Because what?" Lieutenant Ekman asked again.

"Because I wondered if we could stop at the lighthouse on our way home and ask Karen Klasson to go to Stockholm and live with us;" and Gerda held her breath and waited for her father to speak.

"Perhaps she would not like to leave her father and mother for the sake of living with us," he said at last.

"I think she would, if it would make her back well," persisted Gerda.

Herr Ekman laughed. "If living with us would cure people's backs, we might have all the lame children in Sweden to care for," he said.

"But I want only Karen," said Gerda; "and I thought it would be good for her to take the Swedish medical gymnastics at the Institute in Stockholm, where so many people are cured every year."

Lieutenant Ekman looked thoughtfully at his daughter. "That is a good idea and shows a loving heart," he said. "But are you willing to give up any of your pleasures in order to make it possible?"

Gerda looked at him in surprise, and he continued, "I am not a rich man. If we should take Karen into our family and send her to the gymnasium, it would cost a good many kronor, and your mother and I would have to make some sacrifices. Are you willing to make some, too?"

Gerda gazed thoughtfully across the stretches of bog-land to the forest on the horizon. "Yes," she said at last; "I will go without the furs Mother promised to buy for me next winter."

Lieutenant Ekman knew well that Gerda had set her heart on the furs, and that it would be a real sacrifice for her to give them up; but if she were willing to do so cheerfully, it meant that she was in earnest about helping her new friend.

"Yes," he said, after a moment; "if you will give up the furs, we will see what can be done. On the way home we will stop at the lighthouse and ask Hans Klasson to lend Karen to us for a little while."

Gerda clapped her hands. "Oh, a promise! A promise!" she cried joyously. "What a good souvenir of Polcirkel!" and she ran to tell Birger the news.

CHAPTER VI
THE MIDNIGHT SUN

"What time is it, Father?" asked Gerda, as they reached the top of Mount Dundret, and Lieutenant Ekman took the key out of his pocket to open the door of the Tourists' Hut.

"It is half past eleven," replied her father, looking at his watch.

"At noon or at night?" questioned Gerda.

"Look at the sun, and don't ask such foolish questions," Birger told her. "When the sun is high up in the heavens it is noon; but when it is down on the horizon it is night."

Gerda looked off at the sun which hung like a huge red moon on the northern horizon. "Then I suppose it is almost midnight," she said, "and time to go to bed. I was wishing it was nearer noon and dinner-time."

"You'll have to wait for dinner-time and bedtime, too, until we get back to Gellivare," her father told her.

"When you have travelled so far just to see the sun shining at midnight, you should spend all your time looking at it," said Birger, opening his camera to take some pictures.

Gerda looked down into the valleys below, where a thick mist hung over the lakes and rivers; then turned her eyes toward the sun, which was becoming paler and paler, its golden glow shedding a drowsy light over the hills.

"How still it is!" she said softly. "All the world seems to have gone to sleep in the midst of sunshine."

"It is exactly midnight," said her father, looking at the watch which he had been holding in his hand.

Birger closed his camera and slipped it into his pocket. "There," he said, "I have a picture of the sun shining at midnight, to prove to Oscar that it really does shine. Now I am going to gather some flowers to press for Mother;" and he ran off down the side of the hill.

Gerda found a seat on a rock beside the hut, and sat down to watch the beginning of the new day. The sun gradually brightened and became a magnificent red, tinging the clouds with gold and crimson, and gilding the distant hills. A fresh breeze sprang up, the swallows in their nests under the eaves of the hut twittered softly,—all nature seemed to be awake again.

"I've been thinking," said Gerda, after a long silence, "that I told Hilma I should understand about the midnight sun if I should see it; but I'm afraid I don't understand it, after all."

"It is this way," Lieutenant Ekman began. "The earth moves around the sun once every year, and turns on its own axis once every twenty-four hours."

"That is in our geography," Gerda interrupted. "The path which the earth takes in its trip around the sun is called its orbit. The axis is a straight line that passes through the center of the earth, from the North Pole to the South Pole."

"That is right," said her father; "and if old Mother Earth went whirling round and round with her axis perpendicular to her orbit, we should have twelve hours of daylight and twelve hours of darkness all over the earth every day in the year."

"I suppose she gets dizzy, spinning around so fast, and finds it hard to stand straight up and down," suggested Gerda.

"No doubt of it," answered her father gravely. "At least she has tipped over, so that in summer the North Pole is turned toward the sun, but in winter it is turned away from the sun."

"Let me show you how I think it is," said Gerda eagerly. She was always skillful at drawing pictures, and now she took the paper and pencil which her father gave her, and talked as she worked. "This is the sun and this is the earth's orbit," and she drew a circle in the center with a great path around it.

"This is Mother Earth in the summer with the sun shining on her head at the North Pole," and a grandmotherly-looking figure in a Rättvik costume was quickly hung up on the line of the orbit, her head tipped toward the sun.

"Here she is again in winter, with the sun shining on her feet at the South Pole," and Gerda drew the figure on the opposite side of the orbit with her head tipped away from the sun.

"That is exactly how it is," said her father. "But do you understand that, when she is slowly moving round the sun, she is always tipped in the same direction, with the North Pole pointing toward the north star; so there comes a time, twice a year, when her head and her feet are both equally distant from the sun, which shines on both alike?"

"No," said Gerda. "When does that happen?"

"It happens in March and September, when Mother Earth has travelled just half the distance between summer and winter."

"Oh, I see! This is where she would be;" and Gerda made two dots on the orbit, each half-way between the two grandmothers.

"Good," said her father. "Now when she is in that position, day and night, all over the earth, are each twelve hours long. We call them the 'Equinoxes.' It is a Latin word which means 'equal nights.'"

"In March and September do we have a day when it is twelve hours from sunrise to sunset, and twelve hours from sunset to sunrise?" questioned Gerda.

"Yes, and it is the same all over the earth the very same day," repeated Lieutenant Ekman. "If you will look in the almanac when you go home, you will see just which day it is."

Gerda studied her drawing for a few minutes in silence. "I think I understand it now," she said at last.

"It is easy to understand after a little study," her father told her; "but everyone has to see it for himself, just like the midnight sun.

"When the North Pole, or Fru Earth's head, is turned toward the sun we have the long summer days in Sweden. When it is turned away from the sun we have the long winter nights. The nearer we go to the pole, the longer days and nights we have. If we could be directly at the pole, we should have six months of daylight and six months of darkness every year."

"What did you say?" asked Birger, who came around the corner of the hut just in time to hear his father's last words.

"We were explaining how it is that the farther north we go in summer, the longer we can see the sun each day," said Gerda.

"Let me hear you explain it," suggested Birger, trying to find a comfortable seat on the rocky ground.

But Gerda drew a long breath of dismay. "Oh, Birger, you should have come sooner!" she exclaimed. "I understand it perfectly now; but if we go through it again I shall get all mixed up in my mind."

Lieutenant Ekman laughed. "I move that we stay up here and watch the midnight sun until we understand the whole matter and can stand on our heads and say it backwards," he suggested.

"I'm willing to stay all summer, if we can drive off in the daytime and see some Lapp settlements," said Birger, who had made friends with a young Laplander that morning at the Gellivare station.

"But it is daytime all the time!" cried Gerda. "When should we get any sleep?"

"I must be back in Stockholm by the middle of July," said Lieutenant Ekman; "but if your friend knows where there are some Laplanders not too far away, perhaps we can spare time to go and see them."

"Yes, he does," said Birger eagerly. "The mosquitoes have driven most of the herds of reindeer up into the mountains, but Erik's family are still living only a few miles north of Gellivare."

"What is Erik doing in Gellivare?" questioned Herr Ekman.

"He is working in the iron mines," Birger explained. "He wants to save money so that he can go to Stockholm and learn a trade. He doesn't want to stay here in Lapland and wander about with the reindeer all his life."

"So?" said Lieutenant Ekman in surprise. "Your friend Erik seems to have ambitions of his own."

"Look at Gerda!" whispered Birger suddenly.

Gerda sat on the ground with her back against the hut, and she was fast asleep. "Poor child," said her father, as he carried her into the hut and put her on a cot, "she has been awake all night. When she has had a little rest we will go back to Gellivare and look up your friend Erik. After we have all had a good night's sleep, we shall be ready to make a call on his family and their reindeer."

CHAPTER VII
ERIK'S HOME IN LAPLAND

"This is the best part of our trip," Gerda said, two days later, as she was standing in the shade of some fir trees at one of the posting-stations a few miles from Gellivare, waiting for fresh horses to be put into the carts. "I have been reading about Laplanders and their reindeer ever since I can remember, and now I am going to see them in their own home."

"Perhaps you will be disappointed," Birger told her. "Erik says that his father's reindeer may wander away any day to find a place where there is more moss, and if they do, the whole family will follow them."

"Where do they go?" asked Gerda.

"There is a treaty between Norway and Sweden, more than one hundred and
fifty years old, which provides that Swedish Lapps can go to the coast of Norway in summer, and Norwegian Lapps can go inland to Sweden in winter,"
Lieutenant Ekman told the children.

"Yes," said Erik, "when the moss is scanty or the swarms of mosquitoes too thick, the reindeer hurry off to some pleasanter spot, without stopping to ask permission. Perhaps we have been in camp a week, perhaps a month, just as it happens; but when we hear their joints snapping and their hoofs tramping all together, we know it is time to take down the tent, pack up everything and follow the herd to a new pasture."

"I am glad we are out of sight of the photograph shops in Gellivare, anyway," Birger told Erik, when they were seated in the light carts and were once more on their journey. "If I could take such good pictures myself, I shouldn't care; but all my pictures of the midnight sun make it look like the moon in a snow-bank."

Just then Gerda, who was riding with her father, called to Birger, "Stop a moment and listen!" So the two posting-carts halted while the children listened to the music of a mountain stream not far away. Mingled with the sound of the rushing water was the whirr of a busy sawmill in the depths of the woods, while from the tree-tops could be heard the call of a cuckoo and the harsh cry of a woodpecker.

Soon they were on their way again, pushing deeper and deeper through the Lapland forest; their road bordered with green ferns and bright blossoming flowers, their path crossed now and again by fluttering butterflies.

"This is just the right kind of a carriage for such a road, isn't it?" said Gerda, as the track led through a shallow brooklet.

"Yes," answered her father; "a few of the roads in these northern forests are excellent; but many of them are only trails, and are rough and rocky. If the cart were not so light, with only one seat and two wheels, we should often get a severe shaking-up."

"How does it happen that we can get such a good horse and cart up here among the forests?" asked Gerda.

"As there is no railroad in this part of Lapland, the Swedish government very thoughtfully arranges for the posting-stations, and guarantees the pay of the keepers for providing travellers with fresh horses," her father explained. "The stations are from one to two Swedish miles apart, and everyone who hires a horse is expected to take good care of him."

"I'm afraid we shall have to make this horse go faster, or we shall be caught in a thunder-storm," said Gerda, looking up through the trees at the sky, which was growing dark with clouds.

"You are right," answered her father; and at the same moment Erik looked back and shouted, "We must hurry. Perhaps we can reach my father's tent before the rain comes."

Then, glancing up again at the black clouds, he said to Birger, "We shall soon hear the pounding of Thor's hammer."

"How do you happen to know about the old Norse gods?" questioned Birger.

"I have been to school in Jockmock, and I read books," replied Erik, urging on his horse to a race with the clouds; but the clouds won, for the little party had gone scarcely an English mile before they were in the midst of a thunder-storm. Over rocks and rills, under low-hanging boughs of pine and birch trees rattled the carts along the rough woodland road. The rain poured down in sheets, zigzag lightning flashed across the sky, and a peal of thunder crashed and rumbled through the forest.

Lieutenant Ekman threw his coat over Gerda, covering her from head to foot, and called to Erik that they must stop. As he spoke, a second flash of lightning showed a great boulder beside the road and Erik answered, "Here we are at my father's tent. It is just beyond that rock."

Another moment, and with one last jounce and jolt, the two carts had rounded the turn in the road and stopped in a small clearing beside a lake. The arrival of the carts, or kärra, as they are called in Sweden, had brought the whole family of Lapps to the door of the tent. There they stood, huddled together,—Erik's father, mother, brother and sisters,—looking out to see who was arriving in such a downpour.

Lieutenant Ekman jumped down, gathered Gerda up in his arms, coat and all, and ran toward the tent. Birger followed, while Erik waited to tie the horses to a tree.

Immediately the group at the doorway disappeared inside the tent, making way for the strangers to enter, and when Gerda had shaken herself out of her father's coat, a scene of the greatest confusion greeted her eyes.

The frame of the tent was made of poles driven into the ground and drawn together at the top. It was covered with a coarse woolen cloth which is made by the Lapps and is very strong. A cross-pole was fastened to the frame to support the cooking-kettle, under which wood had been placed for a fire.

An opening had been left at the top of the tent to allow the smoke to escape. Birger had often made such a tent of poles and canvas when he was spending the summer with his grandmother in Dalarne.

At the right of the entrance was a pile of reindeer skins, and there, huddled together with the three children, were four big dogs. The dogs stood up and began to growl, but Erik's father, who was a short, thick-set man with black eyes and a skin which was red and wrinkled from exposure to the cold winds, silenced them with a word. He then helped Erik spread some dry skins for the visitors on the left side of the tent.

The Lapp mother immediately busied herself with lighting the fire, putting some water into the kettle to boil, and grinding some coffee. As she moved about the tent, Gerda saw that a baby, strapped to a cradle-board, hung over her back.

The baby's skin was white and soft, her cheeks rosy, her hair as yellow as Gerda's. She opened her blue eyes wide at the sight of the strangers, but not a sound did she make. Evidently Lapp babies were not expected to cry.

The coffee was soon ready, and was poured into cups for the guests, while Erik and his brother and sisters drank theirs in turn from a big bowl.

Lieutenant Ekman talked with Erik's father, who, like many of the Lapps, could speak Swedish; but the children were all silent, and the dogs lay still in their corner, their gleaming eyes watching every motion of the strangers.

When Gerda had finished drinking the coffee, which was very good, she took two small packages from her pocket and put them into her father's hand. "They are for Erik's family," she whispered. "Birger and I bought them in Gellivare."

"Don't you think it would be better for you to give them out yourself?" he asked; but Gerda shook her head as if she had suddenly become dumb, and so Lieutenant Ekman distributed the gifts.

There was a string of shells for the youngest child; a silver ring, a beaded belt, a knife and a cheap watch for the older children; a box of matches and some tobacco for the father, and some needles and bright colored thread for the mother.

"We should like to give you something in return," said Erik's father; "but we have nothing in the world except our reindeer. If we should give you one of them you might have some trouble in taking it home," and he laughed loudly at the idea.

"If you wish to please me, you can do so and help your son at the same time," replied Lieutenant Ekman. "Erik is a good lad. He can read well, and has studied while he has been working in the mines. Now he wishes to learn a trade, and we can take him with us to Stockholm if you will let him go."

Erik's father did not speak for a few moments; then he rose and opened the door of the tent, motioning for the others to follow him out into the forest.

CHAPTER VIII
FOUR-FOOTED FRIENDS

The brief thunder-storm was over, the high noonday sun was shining down into the clearing, and the rumble of Thor's hammer could be heard only faintly in the distance. In the trees overhead the birds were calling to one another, shaking the drops of rain from many a twig and leaf as they flitted among the green branches.

Erik's father took up a stout birch staff which was leaning against the tent, and led the way to the reindeer pasture, followed by his dogs.

These dogs are the useful friends of the Lapps. They are very strong and brave, and watch the reindeer constantly to keep them together. When the herd is attacked by a pack of wolves, the frightened animals scatter in all directions, and then the owner and his dogs have hard work to round them up again.

Now, as the dogs walked along behind their master, they stopped once in a while to sniff the air, and their keen eyes seemed to see everything.

The country was wild and desolate. As far as the eye could reach, there was nothing but low hills, bare and rocky, with dark forests of fir and birch. It was cold and the wind blew in strong gusts. Tiny rills and brooks, formed by the melted snow and the frequent rains, chattered among the rocks; and in the deepest hollows there were still small patches of snow.

Birger gathered up some of the snow and made a snowball. "Put it in your pocket, and take it home to Oscar as a souvenir of Lapland," Gerda suggested.

"No," he replied, taking out his camera, "I'll set it up on this rock and take a picture of it,—snowball in July."

"You'd better wait until you see the reindeer before you begin taking pictures," called Gerda, hurrying on without waiting for her brother. In a few moments more they came in sight of the herd, and saw animals of all sizes, many of them having superb, spreading antlers.

"Look," said Erik's father, pointing to the reindeer with pride, "there are over three hundred deer,—all mine."

"All the needs of the mountain Lapps are supplied by the reindeer," Lieutenant Ekman told the children. "These useful animals furnish their owners with food, clothing, bedding and household utensils. They are horse, cow, express messenger and freight train. In summer they carry heavy loads on their backs; in winter they draw sledges over the snow."

Some of the reindeer were lying down, but others were eating the short, greenish-white moss which grows in patches among the rocks, tearing it off with their forefeet. They showed no signs of fear at the approach of the strangers, and did not even stop to look up at them.

Two or three moved slowly toward Erik when he spoke to them, but not one would touch the moss which he held out in his hand.

"This is my own deer," Erik told Birger, showing a mark on the ear of a reindeer which had splendid great antlers. "He was given to me when I was born, to form the beginning of my herd. I have ten deer now, but I would gladly give them all to my father if he would let me go to Stockholm with you."

Lieutenant Ekman turned to the father. "It shall cost him nothing," he said. "Are you willing that he should go?"

"Yes, if he does not want to stay here," replied the father, who had hoped that the sight of the reindeer would make his son forget his longing to leave home.

Erik nodded his head. "I want to go," he said.

"Then it is settled," said Lieutenant Ekman, "and I will see that he learns a good trade."

"Yes, it is settled," agreed Erik's father; "but I had hoped that my son would live here in Lapland and become an owner of reindeer. There are not so many owners as there should be."

"Why, I thought that all Laplanders owned reindeer!" exclaimed Birger.

"No," said his father, "there are about seven thousand Lapps in Sweden, but only three or four hundred of them own herds. There are the fisher Lapps who live on the coast; and then there are the field Lapps who live on the river-banks and cultivate little farms. It is only the mountain Lapps who own reindeer and spend all their lives wandering up and down the country, wherever their herds lead them."

"What do the reindeer live on in the winter when the snow covers the moss?" questioned Birger.

"The Lapps have to find places where the snow is not more than four or five feet deep, and then the animals can dig holes in the snow with their forefeet until they reach the moss," replied his father. "The reindeer are never housed and seem to like cold weather. They prefer to dig up the moss for themselves, and will not eat it after it has been gathered and dried."

Just then the Lapp mother came to speak to her husband, and in a few minutes all the rest of the family arrived.

"They are going to milk the reindeer," Erik explained to Gerda.

"How often do you milk them?" she asked.

"Twice a week," was the answer. "They give only a little milk, but it is very thick and rich."

Erik and his brother Pers went carefully into the herd and threw a lasso gently over the horns of the deer, to hold them still while the mother did the milking. The twins looked on with interest; but to their great astonishment not one of the reindeer gave more than a mug of milk. They had been used to seeing brimming pails of cow's milk at the Ekman farm in Dalarne.

"How do they ever get enough cream to make butter?" questioned Gerda.

"We never make butter, but we make good cheese," Erik's mother explained, as she brought a cup of milk for them to taste.

"What do these people eat?" Gerda asked her father, when the woman went back to her milking.

"The reindeer furnish them with milk, cream, cheese and meat; and when they sell an animal they buy coffee, sugar, meal, tobacco, and whatever else they need. Then they catch a few fish and kill a bear once in a great while."

"I have killed two bears in my life," Erik's father said with pride. "Look," and he showed his belt, from which hung a fringe of bears' teeth.

"Do all the Lapps know how to speak Swedish?" Birger questioned.

"And do they all know how to read and write?" added Gerda.

Lieutenant Ekman nodded. "Most of them do," he replied. "Our government provides teachers and ministers for the largest settlements, so that the Laplanders may become good Swedish subjects."

"My brother and I went to school in Jockmock last winter," said Erik, who had overheard the conversation. "It is a Lapp village near Gellivare, and my father goes there sometimes to sell toys that we carve from the antlers of the reindeer."

A little five-year-old girl, who had hardly taken her eyes from Gerda's face, suddenly put up her hand and took off a leather pouch which hung around her neck. Opening the pouch, she took from it a tiny bag made of deerskin.

Gerda had noticed that each one of the family wore just such a pouch, and she had seen the mother open hers, when she was making the coffee, and take from it a silver spoon.

From the deerskin bag the child next took a small box made of bone, and by this time Birger and all the others were watching her with interest. Off came the cover of the box. Out of the box came a tiny package wrapped carefully in a bit of woolen cloth, and out of the wrappings came a precious treasure.

"Look," exclaimed Gerda when she saw what it was; "it is a perfect little reindeer!"

And so, indeed, it was,—a tiny animal made from a bit of bone, with hoofs, head and antlers all perfectly carved.

The child held it out toward Gerda, nodding her head shyly to show that she wished to have her take it. But Gerda hesitated to do so until Erik said, "My father will make her another. You gave her the string of shells, and she will not like it if you refuse her gift."

So Gerda took the little reindeer, and many a time in Stockholm, the next winter, she looked at it and thought of the child who gave it to her, and of the curious day she spent with the Lapps in far away Lapland.

CHAPTER IX
KAREN'S BROTHER

"How would you like to spend a whole summer here in the forest, watching the reindeer?" Lieutenant Ekman asked Gerda, after the milking was over and the Lapp mother had gone back to the tent with her children.

"Not very well, if I had to live in that tent," Gerda answered. Then suddenly something attracted her attention, and she held up her hand, saying, "Listen!"

A faint call sounded in the distance,—a call for help.

"This way," cried Erik, and dashed off down a path which led toward the river.

All the others followed him. "It must be one of the lumbermen," said Erik's father. "They often get hurt in the log jams."

He was right. When they reached the riverbank they found several men trying to drive some logs out into the current, so as to release a man who had slipped and was pinned against a rock.

The bed of the river was rilled with rocks, over which the water was rushing with great force, in just such a torrent as may be found on nearly all the rivers of northern Sweden. Starting from the melting snow on the mountains, these rivers flow rapidly down to the sea, and every summer millions of logs go sailing down the streams to the sawmills along the eastern coast.

Thousands of these logs are thrown into the water to drift down to the sea by themselves; but on some of the slower rivers the logs are made up into rafts which are guided down the stream by men who live on the raft during its journey.

It was one of the log-drivers who had been caught while he was trying to push the logs out into the channel; and now his leg was broken.

"We can take him to Gellivare in one of our kärra," said Lieutenant Ekman, when, with the help of Erik and his father, the man had finally been rescued and carried ashore.

Accordingly, he was lifted into the cart with Erik, while Gerda snuggled into the seat between Birger and her father; and the journey over the rough woodland road was made as carefully as possible.

Several interesting things were discovered while the doctor from the mines was setting the broken leg. The most important of all was that this stalwart lumberman had a father who was a lighthouse keeper.

"Ask him if it is the Sea-gull Light," begged Gerda, when she heard of it; "and find out if Karen is his sister."

And it was indeed so. The young man had been in the woods all winter, and was on his way to the lighthouse, which he had hoped to reach in a few days, for the river current was swift and the logs were making good progress down to Luleå.

"You shall reach home sooner than you expected," said Lieutenant Ekman the next morning, "for you shall go with us this very day."

"Fine! Fine! Fine!" cried Gerda joyously when she heard of it. "Pack your bundle, Erik, for you are going with us, too."

While their clothes, and all the little keepsakes of the trip, were being hurried into the satchels, Gerda's tongue flew fast with excitement, and her feet flew to keep it company.

"What do you suppose Karen will say, when she sees us bringing her brother over the rocks?" she ran to ask Birger in one room, and then ran to ask her father in another.

At nine o'clock the injured man was moved into the train, the children took their last look at the mining town, and then began their return over the most northerly railroad in the world, back through the swamps and forests, across the Polcirkel, and out of Lapland.

Luleå was reached at last and Josef Klasson was transported from the train to the steamer, "Just as if he were a load of iron ore from the mines," Birger declared.

"Not quite so bad as that," said his father, and took the twins to see the great hydraulic lift that takes up a car loaded with ore, as easily as a mother lifts her baby, and dumps the whole load into the hold of a vessel.

The children were so full of interest in all the new life around them that Josef Klasson almost forgot his pain in telling them about his winter in the lumber camp, and the long dark night, when for over a month there was not even a glimpse of the sun, and no light except that of the moon and the frosty stars.

It seemed but a very short time before Gerda was crying, "I can see the Sea-gull Light, and Karen is out on the rocks."

Then came all the excitement of landing. The twins told Karen about finding her brother, and the reindeer, and the midnight sun, and the logs in the river, all in one breath; while Lieutenant Ekman explained Josef's accident to the lighthouse keeper and his wife, who had both hurried down to the wharf to find out the meaning of the return of the government boat.

Then, after Josef had been welcomed with loving sorrow because of his injury, and they had carried him up to the house and made him comfortable, Gerda told about her desire to take Karen home with her.

At first the father and mother would not hear of such a thing; but when Herr Ekman told of the medical gymnastic exercises that might cure her lameness, Josef spoke from his cot.

"Let her go," he said. "It is a terrible thing to be lame. These few days that I have been helpless are the worst I have ever known. If there is a chance to make Karen well, let her go."

And so Karen and Erik both went to Stockholm on the boat with Herr Ekman and the twins.

"You know I told you that I never see my brothers very long at one time," Karen said to Gerda, after the children had been greeted and gladly welcomed by Fru Ekman, and they had all tried to make the strangers feel at home among them.

"Yes," said Gerda; "but when you next see Josef you may be so well and strong that you can go off to the lumber camp with him and help him saw down the trees."

Karen shook her head sadly. She could not believe that she would ever walk without a crutch, and it was the first time that she had been away from her mother in all her life. She turned to the window so that Gerda might not see the tears that came into her eyes, and looked down at the strange city sights.

Just then Lieutenant Ekman came into the room. "Oh, Father, may we take Erik to the Djurgård to-morrow?" Birger asked. "I want to show him the Lapp tent and the reindeer out there. He seems to be rather homesick for the forest, and says that we live up in the air like the birds in their nests."

When the four children were asleep for the night, and the father and mother were left alone, they laughed softly together over the situation.

"Who ever heard of bringing a Lapp boy to Stockholm!" exclaimed Herr Ekman; and his wife added, "Who but Gerda would think of bringing a strange child here, to be cured of her lameness?"

CHAPTER X
A DAY IN SKANSEN

It was in the Djurgård that poor Erik first learned that he was a Lapp,—a dirty Lapp.

Of course he knew that his ancestors had lived in Lapland for hundreds of years; but before he went to the Djurgård that day with Birger and Gerda, he had never heard himself called a Lapp in derision.

The Djurgård, or Deer Park, is a beautiful public park on one of the wooded islands near Stockholm. There one finds forests of gigantic oaks, dense groves of spruce, smiling meadows, winding roads and shady paths. Through the tree-branches one catches a glimpse of the blue waters of the fjord, rippling and sparkling in the sun; little steamers go puffing briskly to and fro; and great vessels sail slowly down to the sea.

In summer, steamers and street cars are constantly carrying people back and forth between the Deer Park and other parts of the city. It is not a long trip; from the quay in front of the Royal Palace it takes only ten minutes to reach the park, and day and night the boats are crowded with passengers.

People go there to dine in the open-air restaurants and listen to the bands; they go to walk along the beautiful, tree-shaded paths; or they go to visit Skansen, one of the most interesting museums in the world.

It was to look at the Lapp encampment in Skansen that Birger and Gerda took Erik to the Djurgård. It was to see the birthday celebration in honor of Sweden's beloved poet, Karl Bellman, that they took Karen, for Gerda had already discovered that Karen knew many of Bellman's verses and songs.

The happy little party started early in the afternoon, and as they walked through the city streets, many were the curious glances turned upon the Lapp boy.

Erik wore a suit of Birger's clothes, and although he was five years older, they fitted him well. He was short, as all Lapps are, and his face was broad, with high cheek-bones; but he had a pair of large, honest, black eyes which looked at everybody and everything in a pleasant, kindly way.

"What is that great, upward-going box?" he asked, as he caught sight of the Katarina Hissen, on the quay at the south side of the fjord.

"That is an elevator which will take you up to the heights above, where you can look over the whole city," was Birger's answer. Then he whispered to Gerda to ask if she thought they might go up in the elevator before going to the Deer Park.

Gerda shook her head. "It costs five öre to go up in the lift, and three öre to come down," she replied. "That would be thirty-two öre for us all, and we must save our money to spend in the Djurgård. There is the boat now," and she led the way to the little steamer.

"I have heard you say so much about Skansen," said Karen, when they had found seats on the deck together, "that I'd like to know what it is all about."

"It is all about every old thing in Sweden," laughed Gerda. "The man who planned it said that the time would come when gold could not buy a picture of olden times—the old homes and costumes and ways of living—and then people would wish they could know more about them.

"So he travelled all over Sweden, from one end to the other, making a collection of all sorts of old things to put in a museum in Stockholm. Then he thought of showing the real life of the country people, so he bought houses and set them up in Skansen, and hired the peasants to come and live in them.

"When he finished his work, there was an example of every kind of Swedish dwelling, from the Laplander's tent and the charcoal burner's hut, to the farmhouse in Dalarne and the fisherman's cot in Skåne. And people were living in all the houses just as they had lived at home,—spinning, weaving, baking, and celebrating all the holidays in the same old way."

"And there are cages of wild animals and birds too," added Birger, "polar bears and owls and eagles and reindeer—"

"That is what I want to see,—the reindeer," interrupted Erik; so when the steamer reached the quay at the Deer Park, the children went at once to find the Laplander's tent in Skansen.

Erik stood still for a long time, looking at the rocks, and the Lapps and reindeer; and the twins waited for him to speak. Gerda expected that he would say it was just like home; but, instead, he turned to her at last and asked, "Do you think it is like Lapland?"

The little girl was rather taken aback at his question. "Well, you know, Erik," she stammered, "they have done the best they could."

Erik shook his head. "They could not move the forest, with the rivers and mountains and wild birds," he said. "Without them it is not a real Lapland home."

His whole face said so plainly, "It is only an imitation," that Birger could not help laughing.

"There is no museum in all Europe like Skansen," he said at last, quite proudly; "and there are many people who come here to see it, because they cannot travel, as Gerda and I did, and see the real homes in the country."

"I am one of them," said Karen. "This is the only way I shall ever see a Laplander's tent and reindeer."

"I will show you a house that is just like my grandmother's home in Rättvik," suggested Gerda, and they walked slowly through the woodland paths, so that Karen would not get tired with her crutch.

In a few minutes they came upon a place where some peasants, dressed in their native costumes, were dancing folk-dances; for that is one of the pleasant Skansen ways of saving the old customs.

"Oh, let us stop and look at the dancers!" cried Karen in delight. "I wonder what they are doing," she added, watching their graceful movements forward and back and in and out.

"They are 'reaping the flax,'" said Gerda, who knew all the different dances because she often went to Skansen with her mother and father on sunny summer evenings.

After the flax dance was finished, a company of boys took the platform, and made everyone laugh with a queer, half-comical, half-serious dance which Gerda called the "ox-dance."

"I should like to dance with them," said Erik suddenly.

"Yes, it is a great deal more fun to dance than to watch others," said Gerda kindly; but she moved away from the sight at once, lest Erik should push in among the dancers.

"This is just the time to go over to the Bellman oak," she suggested. "It is the poet's day, and there will be wreaths and garlands hanging on his tree, and a band of music playing some of his songs."

Erik walked along slowly, his eyes looking back longingly toward the dancing, and finally Gerda looked back, too.

"See, Erik," she said, "the boys have finished, and now the girls are going to dance alone. You would not like to dance with the girls;" and then he followed her willingly to the other side of the island.

Crowds of people were gathering under the Bellman oak, and the four children found a seat near-by, where they could see and hear everything that went on around them.

"We must keep Erik here, or else he will insist on going to blow in the band," Gerda whispered to her brother, as she saw the Lapp boy watching the man with the trombone. Then she began to talk about Karl Bellman, the songs and poems he wrote, and how much the people loved him.

"He is one of our most famous poets," she said earnestly, and Erik looked at her and repeated solemnly:—

> "Cattle die,
> Kinsmen die,
> One's self dies, too;
> But the fame never dies,
> Of him who gets a good name."

"Why, Erik!" exclaimed Karen in surprise; "that is from 'The Song of the High' by Odin, the king of the gods. How did you happen to know it?"

"I know many things," said Erik with an air of importance. But there were some things which Erik did not know. One was, how to play the trombone; and it was his strongest trait that he liked to investigate everything that was new and strange.

Now, when Karen spoke in such a tone of admiration, Erik felt that he must find out at once about that queer instrument which made such loud music; and before Gerda knew what he was doing, he had jumped up from the ground and walked to the stand where the musicians were playing.

"Let me try it," he said, and held out his hand for the trombone.

Gerda was in an agony of distress. "Run and get him, Birger," she urged. "Oh, run quick!"

"Erik, Erik, come here!" cried Birger, running after his friend. But before Birger's voice reached his ears, the trombonist had said very plainly and harshly, "Get away from here, you dirty Lapp!" and poor Erik was looking at him with shame and anger in his eyes, when Birger took hold of his clenched hand and led him away from the bandstand.

It was a hard moment for the twins. People were looking at them and laughing, and the words, "Lapp! Lapp!" spoken in a tone of ridicule, could be heard on every side.

"Let us go home," suggested Gerda, her face scarlet with shame at so much unpleasant attention.

"No," said Birger stoutly, "let us stay right here and show that we don't care."

But Karen all at once felt very tired, and when she told Gerda about it, the little party went sadly through the crowd and took their places in silence on the return steamer.

Neither Birger nor Gerda had any heart to tell their friends the names of the different buildings which they saw from the deck of the boat, although Gerda said once, with a brave little effort to make Erik forget his shame, "We will go home through Erik-gatan."

But Erik looked at her with troubled eyes and made no answer. Not until they were safely within the walls of home did he speak, and then it was to ask, "Why did he call me a dirty Lapp?"

"Because many Lapps *are* dirty," replied Birger, feeling just as miserable as Erik looked. "They don't bathe, nor eat from dishes, nor sleep in beds, as good Swedish people do."

"I shall bathe, and eat from dishes, and sleep in beds all the rest of my life," said Erik, his face very white, his eyes very angry. "And I shall learn to use that strange tool that makes loud music," he added.

Lieutenant Ekman stood in the doorway, listening to his words. "Good," he said heartily; "that is the way for you to talk. And you shall learn to use many other tools, too. I have made arrangements to-day for you to work in the ironworks at Göteborg, where they make steamers, engines and boilers. I have a friend there who will look after you, and see that you are taught a good trade."

"But, Father," cried Birger, "Göteborg is a long way from Stockholm! How can Erik go so far alone?"

"I am going over to Göteborg myself next month," replied Inspector Ekman, "and he can go with me. A new lightship is ready to be launched, and I shall have to inspect it and give the certificate before it is accepted by the government."

"Let us go with you! Let us go, too!" begged the twins, dancing round and round their father.

"But what will become of Karen?" he asked.

Gerda and Birger stopped short and looked at their new friend. It was plain to be seen that she was not strong enough to take such a trip.

Fru Ekman put her arm tenderly around the little lame girl. "Karen will visit me," she said kindly.

So it was decided that the twins should go to Göteborg with their father by way of the Göta Canal. When the day for the journey arrived, the satchels were packed once more, and Gerda showed Karen how to water her plants and feed her pet parrot in her absence.

CHAPTER XI
THROUGH THE LOCKS

"What do you think of a girl who goes off on two journeys in one summer?" and Gerda leaned over the railing of the canal-boat to look at her friends on the quay below.

It was the middle of August, and the same group of boys and girls who had seen the twins off to the North in June were now speeding them to the West.

"I think you don't care for Stockholm any longer," called Hilma; while Oscar added, "And you can't care for your friends either, or you wouldn't be leaving them again so soon."

"I shall be home in just seven days," said Gerda, "and if you will all be here on the quay to welcome me, I will tell you the whole story of the wonderful Göta Canal, and our sight-seeing in Göteborg."

"Your friends will have to meet you at the railroad station," her father told her. "We shall come back by train. It is much the quickest way."

"At the railroad station then, one week from to-day," called Gerda, as the steamer backed away from the quay, and swung slowly out into the Mälar Lake.

"Gerda and Birger are the luckiest twins I know," exclaimed Olaf, taking off his cap and swinging it around his head, as he caught sight of Gerda's fluttering handkerchief.

"That boy Erik seems to be very fond of Birger," said Oscar. "And now that the little girl from the lighthouse is going to live with the Ekmans this winter, I suppose the twins will forget all the rest of us."

"Nonsense!" exclaimed Sigrid loyally. "They will never forget their friends. Besides, I like Karen myself. Let's go and see her now. She must be lonely without Gerda."

In the meantime the little party of four—Lieutenant Ekman, with Erik and the twins—were sailing across the eastern end of Lake Mälar toward the Södertelje Canal.

Birger and Gerda explored the boat, making friends with some of the passengers, and then found seats with Erik on the forward deck, where they could see the wooded shore of the lake. They passed many an island with its pretty villas peeping out among the green trees, and saw gay pleasure parties sailing or rowing on the quiet water.

In a short time the boat sailed slowly into the peaceful waters of the Södertelje Canal. This is the first of the short canals which form links between the lakes and rivers of Southern Sweden, thus making a shorter waterway from Stockholm to Göteborg; and while the trip is about three hundred and seventy miles long, only fifty miles is actual canal, more than four-fifths of the distance being covered by lakes and rivers, with a fifty-mile sail on the Baltic Sea.

The principal difficulty in making this waterway across Sweden lay in the fact that the highest of the lakes is about three hundred feet above the sea level, and the boats have to climb up to it from the Baltic Sea, and then climb down to Göteborg. This climbing is accomplished by means of locks in the canals between the different lakes. In some canals there is only one lock, but in others there are several together, like a flight of stairs. There are seventy-six locks in all.

The boat sails into a lock and great gates are closed behind it. Then water pours in and lifts the boat slowly higher and higher until it is on a level with the water in the lock above. The gates in front of the boat are opened, it sails slowly into the next lock, the gates close behind it; and that lock in turn is filled to the level of the one above.

The boat now wound along between the high green banks of the Södertelje Canal until it entered the first of the locks. Birger and Erik ran to the rail to watch the opening and closing of the gates, and the lowering of the boat to the level of the Baltic Sea; but Gerda preferred to talk with some old women who came on board with baskets full of kringlor,—ring-twisted cakes.

The cakes looked so good, and everyone who bought them seemed to find them so delicious, that at last she ran to ask her father for some money; and when the boat had passed the lock and was once more on its way, she presented a bagful of cakes to Birger and Erik.

"The Vikings had no such easy way as this of getting from Lake Mälar out into the Baltic Sea," said Lieutenant Ekman, coming up to find the children, and helping himself generously to the kringlor.

Gerda looked at the gnarled and sturdy oaks that lined the banks of the canal like watchful sentinels. "The Vikings must have loved the lakes and bays of the Northland," she said. "Perhaps they begged All-father Odin to let their spirits come back and make their homes in these trees."

"No doubt they did," replied her father, gravely enough. "I suppose when the trees wave their arms and shake themselves so violently they are saying to each other something like this: 'See how these good-for-nothing children go in good-for-nothing boats over this good-for-nothing ditch.'"

"With their good-for-something father," cried Gerda, throwing her arms around his neck and giving him a loving kiss.

"Am I really good for something?" he asked, as soon as he could speak. "Well then, you must be good for something, too. In olden times the Vikings sailed the seas and brought home many a treasure from foreign shores. See that you take home some treasures from your journey,—something that will remind you of the towns we visit and the sights we see," and he put his hand into his pocket and took out three coins.

"The Vikings had a fashion of taking what they wanted without paying for it," suggested Birger.

"You'd better not try it now, my son," replied Herr Ekman; and he gave each one of the children a krona.

"Here's a kringla to remind me of Södertelje," said Gerda, slipping one of the cakes into her pocket; and then the three children went off to the forward deck to watch the boat sail out into the ocean.

For fifty miles they sailed among wooded islands and rocky ledges, and then entered the canal which connects the Baltic Sea with Lake Roxen. On the way the boat stopped at two or three ports, and each tune the children went ashore to buy a souvenir.

"Show me your treasures, and I will show you mine," Gerda said to Erik, after the first stop.

The boy shook his head. "I bought something useful," he said, "and I shall send it to my father;" but even with coaxing he would not tell what it was, until they were all ready to show their treasures to Lieutenant Ekman. So all three of the children agreed to keep their souvenirs a secret, and had great fun slipping off alone to buy them.

All day and all night, and all the next day, the boat steamed across the open lakes, glided noiselessly into the quiet canals, or climbed slowly step by step up the locks.

Toward night of the second day Birger suddenly announced, "This is Lake Viken, and it is the highest lake on the way between the two ends of the canal route. The captain says that it is more than three hundred feet above the level of the sea."

"Have we seen the prettiest part of the route?" asked Gerda.

"Far from it," was the answer. "The best part of the canal is still before us, at Trollhättan, although the next lake that we enter, Lake Vener, is a lovely sheet of water. It is the largest lake in Sweden, and I must visit one of the lighthouses."

"And I must call upon one of the trolls when we get to Trollhättan," said Gerda, shaking her head with an air of importance.

"I shall walk up the locks," said Birger.

"You mean that you will walk down the locks," Erik corrected him. "After this the boat will go downstairs until we reach the Göta River."

And when, on the last morning of the journey, they reached Trollhättan, with its famous waterfalls and rapids, the children went ashore and left the boat to walk down the steep hillside by itself, while they ran along beside the canal, or took little trips through the groves to get a better view of the falls. Gerda peered under the trees and bushes for a glimpse of the water witches, but she saw not one.

"And now for your treasures," said Lieutenant Ekman, when they were once more on the boat and it was steaming down the Göta River to Göteborg.

"I bought post-cards," Birger announced, and took a handful from his pocket. "Here are pictures of the giant staircase of locks at Trollhättan, Lake Vener at sunset, the fortress at Karlsborg, the castle at Vettersborg, and the great iron works at Motala."

While Herr Ekman was examining the cards and asking Birger all sorts of questions about them, Gerda was busy spreading out her souvenirs on one of the deck chairs; and such a variety as she had! There was a box of soap, a bag filled with squares of beet-sugar, a tiny hammer made in the shape of the giant steam-hammer "Wrath" at Motala, a package of paper made at one of the great paper-mills, lace collars, a lace cap and some beautiful handkerchiefs from Vadstena.

When her father turned his attention to her collection, he held up his hands in amazement. "Are all these things made in Sweden?" he asked. "And did you buy them all with one krona?"

"They are all made in the towns and cities which we have visited," Gerda replied; "but they cost more than one krona. Mother gave me five kronor before we left home and asked me to buy handkerchiefs and laces at Vadstena. They are the best to be found anywhere in Sweden."

"And how about your treasures, Erik?" asked Lieutenant Ekman, after he had admired Gerda's.

Erik put his hand into his coat pocket and took out a box of matches. "These are from Norrköping," he said.

From another pocket he took another box of matches. "And these are from Söderköping," he added. Then from one pocket and another he took boxes of matches of all sizes and kinds, each time naming the town where they were manufactured; while the twins and their father gazed at him in surprise.

"But why so many matches?" asked Lieutenant Ekman, when at last the supply seemed to be exhausted. "You have matches enough there to light the whole world."

"My father will use them to light his fires," replied Erik. "Matches are a great luxury in Lapland.

"And besides," he added, "Sweden manufactures enough matches to light the whole world. The captain told me that they are made in twenty-one different cities and towns, and that they have taken prizes everywhere."

"That is true," said Herr Ekman. "Swedish matches are famous the world over. My young Vikings have each made a good collection of souvenirs."

At that moment a pretty little maid curtsied before them, saying, "Göteborg, if you please."

"Oh dear," sighed Gerda, gathering up her treasures, "here's the end of our long journey over the wonderful canal!"

But Erik looked down the river to the tall chimneys of the iron-works and said to himself, "And here's the beginning of my work in the world."

CHAPTER XII
A WINTER CARNIVAL

"Abroad is good but home is better," quoted Birger, as the railroad train whizzed across the country, bearing the twins toward home once more after four happy days of sight-seeing in Göteborg.

"Vacation will soon be over and we shall be back again in our dear old school," exclaimed Gerda, with a comical expression on her face.

"I feel as if we had been going to the best kind of a school all summer," said her brother, looking out of the window at the broad fields and little red farmhouses cuddling down in the green landscape. "We have been learning about the largest cities, and the canals and railroads, the lakes and rivers, and that is what we have to do when we study geography in school."

"If I ever make a geography," and Gerda gave a great sigh, "I shall have nothing but pictures in it. That is the way the real earth looks outside of the geographies. There are just millions and millions of pictures fitted together, and not a single word said about them."

Birger laughed. "I will study your geography," he said, "if I am not too busy making one of my own."

"What kind of a geography shall you make?" asked Gerda.

"I shall put in my book all my thoughts about the sights I see," he answered. "It will read like this, 'The harbor at Göteborg made me think of Stockholm harbor, with all the different ships that sail away to foreign lands; and of the great world beyond the sea.'"

"Your geography would never please the children half so much as mine," said Gerda; "because we don't all think alike. It makes some people sea-sick when they think of ships."

"Here we are in Stockholm," said Lieutenant Ekman, gathering up the bags and bundles and helping the children out of the train. "Before we write a geography we must see about putting little Karen Klasson under the doctor's care."

But they found that Fru Ekman had already taken Karen to see the doctor, and had made arrangements for her treatment at the Gymnastic Institute.

"The doctor says that I shall be able to walk without a crutch by springtime, if I take the gymnastics faithfully every day," said Karen happily.

"Oh, Gerda," she added, "ever so many of your friends have been to see me. They are such kind boys and girls!"

"Of course they are! They are the best in the world," Gerda declared, and it seemed, indeed, as if there could be no kinder children anywhere than those who filled all the autumn days with the magic of their fun and good-will for the little lame Karen.

Bouquets of flowers, and plants with bright blossoms, simple games, and new books found their way to her room. There was seldom a day when one or another of the friends did not come to tell her about some of their good times, or plan a little pleasure for her; and Karen seemed to find as much enjoyment in hearing of the fun as if she, herself, could really take part in it.

"What is the carnival?" she asked Gerda one evening in late November, when the last of the friends had clattered down the stairs, and the two little girls were sitting beside the tall porcelain stove which filled the room with a comfortable heat. "I have heard you all talking about it for days; but I don't know just what it is."

"It is a day for winter sports, and all kinds of fun, and you shall sit in the casino at the Deer Park and see it for yourself," said Gerda, giving Karen a loving hug.

When the day of the carnival arrived at last, and Karen sat in the casino, cosily wrapped in furs, and looked out over the Djurgård, she knew that she had never dreamed of so much fun and beauty.

There had been heavy hoar frosts for several nights, and the trees had become perfectly white, — the pines standing straight as powdered sentinels, the birches bending under their silvery covering like frozen fountains of spray. The ice was covered with skaters, their sharp steel shoes flashing in the sun, their merry laughter ringing out in the cold, crisp air.

It seemed as if everyone in Stockholm were skating, or snow-shoeing, or skimming over the fields of snow on long skis. Even Fru Ekman, after making Karen comfortable in the casino, strapped a pair of skates on her own feet and astonished the little girl with the wonderful circles and figures she could cut on the ice.

There was no place for beginners in such a company. And indeed, it almost seemed as if Swedish boys and girls could skate without beginning, for many little children were darting about among the crowds of grown people.

Of course Karen's eyes were fixed most often upon the twins, and as they chased each other over the hurdles, or wound in and out among the sail-skaters and long lines of merry-makers, for the first time in her life she had a feeling of envy.

When Gerda left the skaters at last, to sit for a while beside her friend, she saw at once the thought that was in Karen's mind. So, instead of speaking about the fun of skating, she began to talk about the doctor's promise that the lame back would be entirely cured before summer.

"And there is really just as much fun in the summer-time," she said, "for then we can swim, and bathe, and row boats on the lake. You can go to Rättvik with us, too, and then you shall dance and be gayer than any one else."

"Oh, see, there are some men on skis!" cried Karen suddenly, forgetting her feeling of envy in watching the wonderful speed made by the party of ski-runners who came into sight on the crest of the long hill opposite the ice-basin.

The skis, or snow-skates, are a pair of thin strips of hard wood about four inches wide and eight or nine feet long, pointed and curved upward in front. The snow-skater binds one on each foot and glides over the snowy fields, or coasts down the hills as easily as if he were on a toboggan.

"That is the best way in the world to travel over the snow," said Birger, who had come to find Gerda. "See how fast they go!"

Suddenly one of the men darted away from the others, balanced himself for a moment with his long staff, and then shot down the hill like an arrow. A mound of snow six feet high had been built up directly in his path, and as he reached it, he crouched down, gave a spring, and landed thirty or forty feet below, plowing up the light snow into a great cloud, and then slipping on down the hill and out upon the frozen bay.

Many others tried the slide and jump: some fell and rolled over in the snow, others lost off their skis, which came coasting down hill alone like runaway sleds, while others made a long leap with beautiful grace and freedom.

"This method of travelling across country on skis, when there is deep snow, is hundreds of years old," said Fru Ekman, who had come to send the twins away for more fun, while she took her place again beside Karen.

"Men were skiing in Scandinavia as long ago as old Roman times, and Magnus the Good, who defeated the Roman legions, had a company of ski-soldiers. Gustav Vasa organized a corps of snow-skaters, and Gustavus Adolphus used his runners as messengers and scouts."

At that moment there was a sudden commotion outside the door, and a crowd of the skaters came into the casino for some hot coffee, their merry voices and laughter filling the room. Seldom is there gathered together a company of finer men and women, boys and girls, than Karen saw before her. Descendants of the Vikings these were,—golden-haired, keen-eyed and crimson-cheeked.

"Look at that great fellow, taller than all the others," Fru Ekman whispered to Karen. "He is the champion figure-skater of Europe."

"He looks like Baldur, the god of the sun," Karen whispered in reply; and then forgot everything else in watching the gay company.

"I have never seen so many people having such a good time before," she explained to Fru Ekman after a little while. "At the Sea-gull Light there was never anything like this. It is more like the stories of the gathering of the gods, than just plain Sweden.

"I suppose Birger is going to try for a skating prize some day," she added rather wistfully.

Fru Ekman bent and kissed the little girl. "Yes," she answered, "that is why he puts on his skates every day and practices figure-skating on the ice in the canals. But keep a brave heart, little Karen. You, too, shall wear skates some day."

Karen's face lighted up with a happy smile, and a fire of hope was kindled in her heart which made the long hours shorter, and the hard work at the gymnasium easier to bear.

CHAPTER XIII
YULE-TIDE JOYS

It was the day before Christmas,—such a busy day in the Ekman household. In fact, it had been a busy week in every household in Sweden, for before the tree is lighted on Christmas Eve every room must be cleaned and scrubbed and polished, so that not a speck of dirt or dust may be found anywhere.

Gerda, with a dainty cap on her hair, and a big apron covering her red dress from top to toe, was dusting the pleasant living-room; and Karen, perched on a high stool at the dining-room table, was polishing the silver. The maids were flying from room to room with brooms and brushes; and in the kitchen Fru Ekman and the cook were preparing the lut-fisk and making the rice pudding.

The lut-fisk is a kind of smoked fish—salmon, ling, or cod—prepared in a delicious way which only a Swedish housewife understands. It is always the very finest fish to be had in the market, and before it reaches the market it is the very finest fish that swims in the sea. Every fisherman who sails from the west coast of Sweden—and there are hundreds of them—gives to his priest the two largest fish which he catches during the season. It is these fish which are salted and smoked for lut-fisk, and sold in the markets for Christmas and Easter.

When Gerda ran out into the kitchen to get some water for her plants, she stopped to taste the white gravy which her mother was making for the lut-fisk.

Then as she danced back through the dining-room to tell Karen about the pudding she sang:—

> "Away, away to the fishers' pier,
> Many fishes we'll find there,—Big salmon,
> Good salmon:
> Seize them by the neck,
> Stuff them in a sack,
> And keep them till Christmas and Easter."

"Hurry and finish the silver," she added, "and then we will help Mother set the smörgåsbord for our dinner. We never had half such delicious things for it before. There is the pickled herring your father sent us, and the smoked reindeer from Erik's father in Lapland; and Grandmother Ekman sent us strawberry jam, and raspberry preserve, and cheese, and oh, so many goodies!" Gerda clapped her hands so hard that some of the water she was carrying to her plants was spilled on the floor. "Oh, dear me!" she sighed, "there is something more for me to do. We'd never be ready for Yule if it wasn't for the Tomtar."

The Tomtar are little old men with long gray beards and tall pointed red caps, who live under the boards and in the darkest corners of the chests. They come creeping out to do their work in the middle of the night, when the house is still, and they are especially helpful at Christmas time.

The two little girls had been talking about the Tomtar for weeks. Whenever Karen found a mysterious package lying forgotten on the table, Gerda would hurry it away out of sight, saying, "Sh! Little Yule Tomten must have left it."

And one day when Gerda found a dainty bit of embroidery under a cushion, it was Karen's turn to say, "Let me have it quick! Yule Tomten left it for me." Then both little girls shrieked with laughter.

Birger said little about the Tomtar and pretended that he did not believe in them at all; but when Gerda set out a dish of sweets for the little old men, he moved it down to a low stool where they would have no trouble in finding it.

But now the Tomtar were all snugly hidden away for the day, so Gerda had to wipe up the water for herself, and then run back to her dusting; but before it was finished, Birger and his father came up the stairs,—one tugging a fragrant spruce tree, the other carrying a big bundle of oats on his shoulder.

"Here's a Christmas dinner for your friends, the birds," Birget told Karen, showing her the oats.

For a moment Karen's chin quivered and her eyes filled with tears, as she thought of the pole on the barn at home where she had always fastened her own bundle of grain; but she smiled through her tears and said cheerfully, "The birds of Stockholm will have plenty to eat for one day at least, if all the bundles of grain in the markets are sold."

"That they will," replied Birger. "No one in Sweden forgets the birds on Christmas day. You should see the big bundles of grain that they hang up in Rättvik."

"Come, Birger," called his father from the living-room, "we must set up the tree so that it can be trimmed; and then we will see about the dinner for the birds."

Gerda and Karen helped decorate the tree, and such fun as it was! They brought out great boxes of ornaments, and twined long ropes of gold and gleaming threads of silver tinsel in and out among the stiff green branches. They hung glittering baubles upon every sprig, and at the tip of each and every branch of evergreen they set a tiny wax candle, so that when the tree was lighted it would look as if it grew in fairyland.

But not a single Christmas gift appeared in the room until after all three children had had their luncheon and gone to their rooms to dress for the afternoon festivities. Even then, none of the packages were hung upon the tree. Lieutenant Ekman and his wife sorted them out and placed them in neat piles on the table in the center of the room, stopping now and then to laugh softly at the verses which they had written for the gifts.

"Will the daylight never end!" sighed Gerda, looking out at the red and yellow sky which told that sunset was near. Then she tied a new blue ribbon on her hair and ran to help Karen.

"The postman has just left two big packages," she whispered to her friend. "I looked over the stairs and saw him give them to the maid."

"Perhaps one is for me," replied Karen. "Mother wrote that she was sending me a box."

"Come, girls," called Birger at last; "Father says it is dark enough now to light the tree." And so it was, although it was only three o'clock, for it begins to grow dark early in Stockholm, and the winter days are very short.

All the family gathered in the hall, the doors were thrown open, and a blaze of light and color met their eyes from the sparkling, shining tree. With a shout of joy the children skipped round and round it in a merry Christmas dance, and even Karen hopped about with her crutch.

The cook in her white apron, and the maids in their white caps, stood in the doorway adding their chorus of "ohs!" and "ahs!" to the general excitement; and then, after a little while, the whole family gathered around the table while Herr Ekman gave out the presents.

It took a long time, as there were so many gifts for each one, and with almost every gift there was a funny rhyme to be read aloud and laughed over. But no one was in a hurry. They wondered and guessed; they peeped into every package; they admired everything.

When the last of the gifts had been distributed, there was the dinner, with the delicious lut-fisk, the roast goose, and the rice pudding. But before it could be eaten, each one must first taste the dainties on the smörgåsbord,—a side-table set out with a collection of relishes.

There was a tiny lump in Karen's throat when she ate a bit of her mother's cheese; but she swallowed them both bravely, and was as gay as any one at the dinner table.

All the boys and girls in Sweden are sent to bed early on Christmas Eve. They must be ready to get up the next morning, long before daylight, and go to church with their parents to hear the Christmas service and sing the Christmas carols. So nine o'clock found Karen and the twins gathering up their gifts and saying good-night.

"Thanks, thanks for everything!" cried the two little girls, throwing their arms around Fru Ekman's neck; and Karen added rather shyly, "Thanks for such a happy Christmas, dearest Tant."

"But this is only Christmas Eve," Gerda told her, as they scampered off to bed. "For two whole weeks there will be nothing but fun and merriment. No school! No tasks! Nothing to do but make everyone joyous and happy everywhere. Yule-tide is the best time of all the year!"

CHAPTER XIV
SPURS AND A CROWN

"Rida, rida, ranka!
  The horse's name is Blanka.
Little rider, dear and sweet,
Now no spurs are on your feet;
When you've grown and won them,
Childhood's bliss is done then.

 "Rida, rida, ranka!
  The horse's name is Blanka.
Little one with eyes so blue,
A kingly crown will come to you,
A crown so bright and splendid!
Then youthful joy is ended."

Fru Ekman sang the words of the old Swedish lullaby as she had sung them many times, years before, when the twins lay in their blue cradle at Grandmother Ekman's farm in Dalarne; but now the boy stood proudly in a suit of soldier gray, and the girl made a pretty picture in a set of soft new furs.

It was the morning of the twins' twelfth birthday, and a March snowstorm was covering the housetops and pavements with a white fur coat, "Just like my own pretty coat," Gerda said, turning slowly round and round so that everyone might see the warm white covering.

"The snow will soon be gone," she added, "but my furs will wait for me until next winter."

"You may wear them to school to-day in honor of your birthday," said her mother; "but Birger's soldier suit seems a little out of season."

Birger had taken a fancy to have a suit of gray with black trimmings, such as the Swedish soldiers wear, and it had been given to him with a new Swedish flag, as a match for Gerda's furs.

Lieutenant Ekman turned his son around in order to see the fit of the trim jacket. "When you get the gun to go with it," he told the lad, "you will be a second Gustavus Adolphus."

"If I am to be as great a man as Gustavus Adolphus, I shall have to go to war," replied Birger; "and there seems to be little chance for a war now."

"There are many peaceful ways by which a man may serve his country," Lieutenant Ekman told his son; "but King Gustavus II had to fight to keep Sweden from being swallowed up by the other nations."

"I could never understand how Sweden happened to have such a great fighter as Gustavus Adolphus," said Karen; but Gerda shook a finger at her.

"Sh!" she said, "that isn't the way to talk about your own country. And have you forgotten Gustav Vasa? He was the first of the Vasa line of kings; and he and Gustavus Adolphus and Charles XII made the name of Vasa one of the most illustrious in Swedish history."

"Karen will never forget Gustav Vasa," said Birger, "after she has been to Dalarne and seen all the places where he was in hiding before he was a king."

"Yes," said Gerda, "there's the barn where he worked at threshing grain, and the house where the woman lowered him out of the window in the night, and the Stone of Mora, on the bank of the river, where he spoke to the men of Dalarne and urged them to fight for freedom."

"And there's the stone house in Mora over the cellar where Margit Larsson hid him when the Danish soldiers were close on his track," added Birger. "The inscription says: —

"'Gustav Eriksson Vasa, while in exile and wandering in Dalarne with a view of stirring up the people to fight for Fatherland and Freedom, was saved by the presence of mind of a Dalecarlian woman, and so escaped the troops sent by the Tyrant to arrest him.

"'This monument is gratefully erected by the Swedish people to the Liberator.'"

Karen laughed. "How can you remember it so well?" she asked. "It sounded as if you were reading it."

"That is because I have read it so often," replied Birger. "Gustav Vasa is my favorite hero. He drove the Danes out of the country and won freedom for the Swedish people."

"He was the Father of his Country," said Gerda, and she seized Birger's new flag and waved it over her head.

"Come, children, it is time for you to go to school," Fru Ekman told them; and soon Karen was trudging off to her gymnastic exercises, and the twins were clattering down the stairs with their books.

"That was a good song that Mother was singing this morning," Birger told his sister. "I'd like to wear spurs on my feet. How they would rattle over these stone pavements!"

"I'd rather have 'a crown so bright and splendid,'" said Gerda; "but I'll have to be contented with my cooking-cap to-day instead." Then she bade her brother good-bye and ran up the steps of the school-house, where, after her morning lessons, she would spend an hour in the cooking-class.

At five o'clock the three children were all at home again, and dressed for the party which the twins had every year on their birthday.

"It is time the girls and boys were here," said Gerda, standing before the mirror in the living-room to fasten a pink rose in the knot of ribbon at her throat.

"Here they come!" cried Birger, throwing open the door, and the twelve children who had come before, bringing packages for the surprise box, came again, — this time with little birthday gifts for the twins.

For an hour there was the greatest confusion, with a perfect babel of merry voices and laughter. The gifts were opened and admired by everyone. Gerda put on her fur coat and cap, Birger showed a fine new pair of skates which his father had given him, and Karen brought out a box of little cakes which her mother had sent for the party.

But when the children formed in a long line and Fru Ekman led the way to the dining-room, their excitement knew no bounds.

The table was a perfect bower of beautiful flowers. There was a bouquet of bright blossoms at every plate, and long ropes of green leaves and blossoms were twined across the table, in and out among the dishes. At Gerda's place there was a wreath of violets, with violet ribbons on knife, fork and spoon; a bunch of violets was tucked under her napkin, and a big bow of violet ribbon was tied on her chair.

Birger's flowers were scarlet pinks, with scarlet ribbons and a scarlet bow; and at the two ends of the table were the two birthday cakes, almost hidden among flowers and wreaths, with Birger's name on one and Gerda's on the other, done in colored candies set in white frosting.

Another happy hour was spent at the table, and then the guests trooped away to their homes, leaving the twins to look over their gifts once more.

But the best gift was still to come,—a never-to-be-forgotten gift that came on that wonderful night of their twelfth birthday.

All day there had been a strange feeling in the air. When the girls brushed their hair in the morning it was full of tiny sparkles and stood out from their heads like clouds of gold, and Birger had found, early in the day, that if he stroked the cat's fur it cracked and snapped like matches, much to Fru Kitty's surprise.

Now, when Gerda went to look out of the window, she called to the others to come quickly to see the northern lights; for out of the north there had come a gorgeous illumination, filling the heavens with a marvellous radiance such as only the aurora borealis can give.

Banners of crimson, yellow and violet flamed and flared from horizon to zenith; sheets of glimmering light streamed across the sky, swaying back and forth, and changing from white to blue and green, with once in a while a magnificent tongue of red flame shooting higher than the others.

"It is a carnival of light," said Gerda, in a tone of awe. She had often seen the northern lights, but never any so brilliant as these.

Everyone seemed charged with the electricity, and little Karen said softly, "I never felt so strange before. The lights go up and down my back to the tip of my toes."

"It is the elves of light dancing round the room," said Birger with a laugh.

"No," said Gerda, "it is the Tomtar playing with the electric wires."

Then, as they all stood watching the wonderful display in the heavens, the door opened and Lieutenant Ekman came into the room. "Here is a letter for Karen from her mother," he said; "I have had it in my pocket all day."

"Oh, let me see it," said Karen, and she turned and ran across the room. Yes, ran,—with her crutch standing beside the chair at the window, and her two feet pattering firmly on the floor.

"Look at Karen," cried Gerda. "She has forgotten her crutch!"

Karen held her mother's letter in her hand, and her two eyes were shining like stars. "I feel as if I should never need my crutch again," she said. Then she turned to Fru Ekman and asked breathlessly, "Do you believe that I will?"

"I am sure that you won't," replied Fru Ekman, stooping to kiss the happy child. "I have noticed for a long time that your back was growing straighter and stronger, and you were walking more easily."

Gerda clapped her hands and ran to throw her arms around her friend. "Oh, Karen," she exclaimed, "this is the best birthday gift of all! The Tomtar sent it on the electric wires."

"No," said Birger, "it was the elves of light dancing across the room."

But Karen looked at the little family clustered so close around her. "It is my crown of joy and is from each one of you," she said; "but from Gerda most of all."

CHAPTER XV
THE MIDSUMMER FESTIVAL

It was the middle of June. School was over and vacation had begun. Gerda and Birger were on their way to Rättvik, taking Karen with them so that she might see the great midsummer festival before going to spend the summer at the Sea-gull Light.

"Isn't this the best fun we ever had, — to be travelling alone, without any one to take care of us?" asked Birger, as the train whizzed along past fields and forests, lakes and rivers.

"It feels just as if we were tourists," replied Gerda, straightening her hat and nestling close to Karen.

Karen dimpled and smiled. "I don't see your wonder-eyes, such as tourists always have," she said.

"That is because we have been to Rättvik so many times that we know every house and tree and rail-fence along the way," answered Birger. "We have stopped at Gefle and seen the docks with their great piles of lumber and barrels of tar; and we have been to Upsala, the ancient capital of Sweden, and seen the famous University which was founded fifteen years before Columbus discovered America."

"Last summer Father took us to Falun to visit the wonderful copper mines," added Gerda; "but I never want to go there again," and she shivered as she thought of the dark underground halls and chambers.

"We saw a fire there, which was lighted hundreds of years ago and has never once been allowed to go out," said Birger. "The miners light their lamps and torches at the flame."

"Look, there are the chimneys of Falun now," cried Gerda, pointing out of the car window; and a half-hour later the children found themselves at the neat little Rättvik station.

"Six o'clock, and just on time," said Grandmother Ekman's cheerful voice, and the next moment all three were gathered in a great hug.

"Is there room for triplets in your house?" asked Gerda. "We have outgrown our twinship now, and there are three of us, instead of two."

"There is enough of everything, for Karen to have her good share," said the grandmother heartily; and they were soon driving along the pleasant country road, toward the red-painted farmhouse and the quiet living-room where the tall clock was still ticking cheerfully.

The next morning, and the next, the twins were up bright and early to show Karen all their favorite haunts; and the days flew by like minutes.

"Don't you love it, here in Rättvik, Karen dear?" asked Gerda, on the third day, as the two little girls were busily at work in the pleasant living-room.

"Yes," replied Karen; "but you never told me half enough beautiful things about it. Surely there can be no lovelier place in the whole world than the mill-pool where we went yesterday with Linda Nilsson."

Karen was coloring the letters in a motto to hang on the wall: and Gerda, who was weaving a rug on her grandmother's wooden loom, crossed the room to admire her friend's work. She leaned against Karen's chair and read the words of the motto aloud: "To read and not know, is to plow and not sow."

"That is Grandmother Ekman's favorite motto," she said. "She believes that a burning, golden plowshare was dropped from heaven ages ago, in the beginning of Sweden's history, as a symbol of what the gods expected of the people; and she says that a well-kept farm and a well-read book are the most beautiful things in the world."

Birger looked up from the door-step where he was whittling out a mast for one of his boats. "If I didn't intend to be an admiral in the navy when I am a man," he said, "I should come here and take care of the farm. It really is the prettiest farmhouse and the best farm in Dalarne."

"It certainly will be the prettiest by night, when we have it dressed up for the midsummer festival," Gerda declared. "Come, Birger! Come, Karen! We must go and gather flowers and birch leaves to decorate the house."

"But we must put away our work first," said orderly Karen, gathering up her paints and brushes.

Gerda ran to push the loom back into the corner. As she did so, she said with a smile, "The first rug I ever made was very ugly. It had a great many dark strips in it. That was because my grandmother made me weave in a dark strip every time I was naughty."

Karen laughed. "How I would like to see it," she said.

"Oh, I have it now. I will show it to you," and Gerda crossed the room and opened one of the chests which were ranged against the wall.

"This is my own chest, where my grandmother keeps everything I make," she said, as she lifted the cover and took out a bundle. Opening the bundle, she unrolled a funny little rug.

Pointing to a wide black stripe in the middle, Gerda said, "That was for the time I broke the vinegar jug, and spoiled Ebba Jorn's dress."

"Oh, tell me about it!" cried Karen.

"No," replied Gerda, "it was too naughty to tell about;" and she put the rug quickly back into the chest.

"I didn't know you were ever naughty," said Karen, laughing merrily. Then, as the two little girls put on their caps and took up their baskets to go flower-hunting, she asked, "Who is Ebba Jorn?"

"She lives across the lake, and she is going to be married to-morrow," answered Gerda. "We can walk in her procession."

Karen gave a little gasp of pleasure. "Oh, what fun!" she exclaimed. Then she stopped and looked down at her dress. "But I have nothing to wear," she said. "All my prettiest dresses went home on the steamer with your father."

"We shall wear our rainbow skirts," Gerda told her. "And you can wear one of mine."

Just then she caught sight of a crowd of boys and girls in a distant meadow, and ran to join them; calling to Birger and Karen to come, too. "They are gathering flowers to trim the Maypole for the midsummer festival," she cried.

It is small wonder that the people of the Northland joyously celebrate the bright, sunny day of midsummer, after the cold days and long dark nights of winter. It is an ancient custom, coming down from old heathen times, when fires were lighted on all the hills to celebrate the victory of Baldur, the sun god, who conquered the frost giants and the powers of darkness.

On Midsummer's Eve, the twenty-third of June, a majstång is erected in every village green in Sweden. The villagers and peasants, young and old, gather from far and near, and dance around the May-pole all through the long night, which is no night at all, but a glowing twilight, from late sunset till early dawn.

There was a great deal of work to be done in preparation for this festival, and such a busy day as the children had! They gathered basketfuls of flowers, and long streamers of ground pine, which they made into ropes and wreaths. They cut great armfuls of birch boughs, and decorated the little farmhouse, inside and out; placing the graceful branches with their tender green leaves wherever there was a spot to hold them. Over the doors and windows, up and down the porch, along the fence, and even around the well, they twined the long ropes and fastened the green wreaths and boughs.

After a hasty lunch they rowed across the lake and spent the afternoon at the village green, helping to dress the tall majstång; and when their supper of berries and milk and caraway bread was eaten, they were glad enough to tumble into bed, although the sun was till shining and would not set until nearly eleven o'clock.

"Wait until to-morrow," murmured Gerda drowsily; "then you will see the happiest day of the whole year."

Karen tried to tell her that every day was happy, now that she could run and play like other children; but she fell asleep in the middle of the sentence, and Gerda hadn't even heard the beginning of it.

"The sun has been dancing over the hills for hours," called Grandmother Ekman at five o'clock the next morning. "It is time for everyone to be up and making ready for church."

All the festival days in Sweden begin with a church service, and everyone goes to church. In the cities the people walk or ride in street-cars or carriages; but in Dalarne some ride on bicycles, some drive, some sail across the lake in the little steamer, and others row in the Sunday boat.

Grandmother Ekman always followed the good old custom of rowing with her neighbors in the long boat, and six o'clock found her at the wharf with the three children, all carrying a beautiful branch of white birch with its shining green leaves.

"This is just what I have wanted to do, ever since you told me about it at the Sea-gull Light," whispered Karen, as they found seats in the boat and began the pleasant journey across the peaceful, shining water.

Gerda was in a great state of excitement. She discovered so many things to chatter about that Grandmother Ekman said at last, "Hush, child! You must compose yourself for church and the Bible reading."

Then Gerda became sober at once, and sat quietly enough during the service, until she fell to thinking how lovely the May-pole would look in its gala dress of green, red, yellow and white.

"It will be wearing a rainbow skirt, like all the girls in the village," she thought; and surprised her grandmother by smiling in the midst of the sermon, at the thought of how very tall this Maypole maiden would be.

The May-pole is always the tallest, slenderest tree that can be found, and the one which Gerda and Karen had helped to decorate was at least sixty feet from base to tip. It had been brought from the forest by the young men of the village, and trimmed of its bark and branches until it looked like the mast of a vessel. Hoops and crosspieces reaching out in every direction were fastened to the pole, and it was then decorated with flowers, streamers, garlands and tiny flags.

Now it was leaning against the platform in the village green, not far from the church, where it was to be raised after the service.

When Gerda and Karen reached the green they found a group of young people gathered about the pole, tying strings of gilded hearts, festoons of colored papers, and fluttering banners to its yard-arms.

"Now it is ready to be raised!" shouted Nils Jorn at last, and everybody fell away to make room for the men who were to draw it into its place with ropes and tackle.

"Suppose it should break!" gasped Karen, and held her breath while it rose slowly in the air. As it settled into the deep hole prepared for it, Nils Jorn waved his cap and shouted. Then some one else shouted, and soon everybody was shouting and dancing, and the festival of the green leaf had begun.

All day and all night the fun ran high, with singing and dancing and feasting.

When there was a lull in the merriment, it was because a long procession had formed to accompany the bride and bridegroom to the church. After the ceremony was over, and the same procession had accompanied them to the shore of the lake, some one called out, "Now let us choose a queen and crown her, and carry her back to the May-pole where she shall decide who is the best dancer."

Oh, it was a hard moment for many of them then, for every maiden hoped that she would be the one to be chosen. But Nils Jorn caught sight of Gerda's merry smile, and nodded toward her.

"Gerda Ekman has seen plenty of dancing in Stockholm," he said. "Let her be our queen."

"Yes, yes!" shouted the others; and for a moment it looked as if Gerda would, indeed, have her wish to wear a crown. But when she saw Karen's wistful look, she turned quickly to her friends and said, "Let me, instead, choose the queen; and I will choose Karen Klasson. I want this to be the happiest day of all the year for her."

"One queen is as good as another," said Nils Jorn cheerfully; so they led Karen back to the May-pole and she was made queen of the festival and crowned with green leaves.

After a few minutes Gerda found a seat beside her under the canopy of birch boughs, and the two little girls watched the dancing together.

Everyone was happy and jolly. The fiddler swept his bow across the strings until they sang their gayest polka. The accordion puffed and wheezed in its attempt to follow the merry tune. The platform was crowded with dancers, whirling and stamping, turning and swinging, laughing and singing.

The tall pole quivered and shook until all the streamers rustled, all the flags fluttered, and all the birch leaves murmured to each other that summer had come and the sun god had conquered the frost giants.

"This is truly the happiest day of all my life," Karen said; "and it is you, Gerda, who have made it so. I was lame and lonely in the cold Northland, and you came, bringing me health and happiness."

"Mother says I must never forget that I was named for the goddess who shed light and sunshine over the world," replied Gerda soberly. Then she drew her friend closer and whispered, "But think, Karen, of all the good times we shall have next year, when you can go to school with me, and we can share all our happiness with each other;" and she clapped her hands and whirled Karen off into the crowd of dancers,—the gayest and happiest of them all.